Chris Meckley
1982

=Wife===
Found Slain

Wife Found Slain

Caroline Crane

DODD, MEAD & COMPANY
NEW YORK

=Wife=
Found Slain

1

She woke slowly, feeling her way in a world of unconnected sounds. From somewhere far off, she heard voices. The clank of something metallic. Brisk footsteps.

At first none of it meant anything. After a while she became conscious of herself, of her body. She was lying on her back and she was in pain.

She tried to define the pain. It was everywhere.

Dimly she sought an explanation. Perhaps there wasn't one. This might have been the way it was supposed to be and always had been.

But that couldn't be true. She could not have borne it always. She could scarcely take a breath without being stabbed. Her face was a mass of agony.

I hurt.

That was her identity—the pain.

There must have been more. Gradually the fog drifted from her mind, leaving her better able to think, if not remember. She groped for something to hold to, something that would tell her more about herself than just the pain.

Her eyes had been closed. She forced them open. Only the left one obeyed. The right was stiff, or stuck. She caught a glimpse of her eyelashes, magnified.

She stared at the ceiling, at the cream-color wall, and the bright, curtainless window beside her bed. She lay with her head and knees slightly raised. There was a railing on either side of her. She was in a hospital.

Outside the window she could see blue sky. Nothing else. It was a pale, whitish blue, like the last time she had seen it. When was that? She remembered the sky. And something had happened.

She reached back, trying to remember more. She saw pictures, faces, but did not know what to make of them. She gave it up and closed her eyes. It was better that way, better to disappear completely, back to where she had been before she woke.

Something rustled nearby. Again she opened her eyes and tried to turn her head.

It had been only a small sound, but it jarred her into alertness. She did not know why.

She was in danger. Her nerves hummed like electric wires, sending messages of fear and pain.

She watched for a while and saw nothing but a half-open door. It did not move, and no one appeared.

As her fear ebbed, she thought how odd it was to be in a place and not know how she got there. She must have been unconscious.

It had something to do with the car. She remembered the car, and seeing the sky. And frozen ground.

She allowed her mind to float and concentrated on her body. Her hands, although bandaged, were movable. Her face was a mammoth ache. Her legs . . .

They seemed all right, but her torso was stiff. Rigid. With the fingers of her left hand, which protruded from their bandage, she felt a wrapping on her chest. Broken ribs.

Her eyes closed and again she felt the car rushing out of control. She moaned, wanting to scream. *Owen!* Where was Owen?

She could not remember the crash. Perhaps it hadn't happened yet.

Of course it had happened, if she was here in a hospital. She could not remember whether Owen had been with her in the car. Was he hurt?

She could not remember whether she was Owen's wife. There had been someone else. Someone named . . .

It was a short name. Something like Rose. Or Ruth.

That was it. Ruth. But Ruth, she thought, was gone. She had an odd sense of finality about it, as though probably Ruth was dead.

It was strange that she should remember Ruth's name and not her own.

Again she tried to relate herself to something or someone. She began with Owen. But she did not know where he was or when she had last seen him.

And the children. The twins, Neal and Paul.

There were others, too. Ruth's children. Eddie? No, Eddie was her own brother. There was a boy, and then that terrible girl who hated her.

She floated again, and wondered whether she had dreamed it all. Owen's children. How did she know them? They were out on Long Island with Ruth.

A whirring sound roused her. A young man had come into the room, pushing a vacuum cleaner or floor polisher, she could not see which.

"Afternoon," he said, and looked away quickly.

My face, she thought. *He can't stand my face.*

Painfully she raised her left hand and felt the face with her fingertips.

Bandages, and skin. It was not completely covered. If she had been burned, at least some of her remained.

I must look horrible. She tried to feel what was there. Her nose. Eyelashes.

The young man stole another look at her. Then he vanished beyond where she could see him. When he reappeared, he was watching her again.

Would this be her life? Would they all stare at her ugly face?

And Owen. He used to say she was pretty. How would he feel about her now? Again she touched her face. She would have liked to know what was wrong with it, whether she would be scarred.

The young man was beginning to upset her. She closed her eyes and waited for him to leave.

She did not know she had fallen asleep until she woke to feel someone bending over her.

She started violently.

It was only a nurse. She relaxed, paying for her alarm with new pain.

The nurse spoke in a soothing voice. "It's all right, Mrs. Holdridge, nothing to worry about. The doctor's here to see you."

Mrs. Holdridge? That was Owen's name. Then she was right. She and Owen . . .

But what's *my* name? she wanted to ask, and found she could not move her mouth.

The doctor pulled a chair over to her bed and sat down. He was a handsome man, with wavy hair and long sideburns. He took her face between his hands and gently turned it. She winced.

"Quite a knock you got there," he said. "I wish you could tell me what happened. We've had to tie up your mouth for a while, so you're going to get lessons in how to live with a wired jaw."

He talked to her as though she were a child. She could relax and let him take care of her.

"We'll have to keep you on a liquid diet for now," he went on. "Even that might give you a little trouble, with the swelling around your mouth, so don't be afraid to ask for help. I'll put the call button here beside you."

He dropped something gray onto the bed next to her pillow. She would have a hard time asking for anything, with a mouth that would not move.

He pulled down the sheet and ran his fingers over the bandages on her chest.

"They tell me you got it worse than the car did," he said, "even though you were inside the car. That's pretty unusual. And these fractures and contusions aren't what I'd have expected under the circumstances. Did you have a fall just before the accident? Did you fall downstairs, maybe? Land on your face?"

Maybe she had. And maybe Owen had been taking her to the hospital, and they crashed. But where was Owen now? Why wouldn't they tell her?

She tried to shake her head, to answer that she did not know. Pain shot through her neck. The immobility of her mouth, the doctor had said, was because her lips were bruised and swollen. How did he expect an answer? She lifted her left hand, the only one she could manage, and moved it back and forth in a negative gesture.

She could not remember. She really could not remember what had happened. The only thing she knew was that there were no stairs she could have fallen down. The garage—

Or was it the off-street parking area at her apartment? Where had she been? If only someone would tell her who she was and where she lived.

It was out in the country somewhere. That house on a hill.

No, that was Ruth's house. She knew, because she had driven by once and seen it.

She wished they would go away. She was tired. Being adrift was exhausting. She needed an anchor, an identity.

And they had no way of knowing that she didn't know who she was or what had happened to her.

The doctor stood up, his hands in his pockets.

"I'd like to find out more about this. As soon as that swelling goes down, we'll talk again."

He and the nurse went out together. She heard the nurse ask a question, but did not hear the words.

She had wanted them to leave, but now that they were

gone, she wished they would come back. It frightened her to be alone. She was afraid of something, and did not know what it was.

She closed her eyes again and tried to remember where she had been when it happened. She tried to remember all the places where she had ever been, hoping she would recognize the one. None seemed to stand out, none was more than far off and hazy. She began to wonder if she was really anybody at all.

She started at the sound of voices in the corridor, rapidly approaching. Before she could turn her head, they had passed her doorway and gone.

By moving only her eyes, she could see almost all the way around the room. It was small and had only one bed. A private room. She wondered who was paying for it.

And then the fear began to seep back. She was alone, with no one to protect her. No one who could call for help.

Somewhere down the corridor, she heard the clink of dishes. It occurred to her that she had no idea what time it was. Or what day, or even which season. She wondered what it would be like to wake from a coma and discover that it was five or ten years later.

The sounds of dishes and voices came closer. A large woman in a green uniform padded softly into the room and deposited a tray on the bedside table.

"Some lunch for you, dear."

She did not want lunch. She only wanted to be rid of the pain. To know who she was, and to be loved by Owen.

Got to get out of here, she thought. Get out and not be alone.

She tried to sit up. Hot knives seared her chest. She flopped back and thought: I'm going to die in this place.

After a while a nurse came in, pressed a button at the side of the bed, and raised it to a sitting position.

"I'm sorry you had to wait. You must be hungry by now."

She could not bear the thought of food, even a liquid. And when was "by now"? In relation to what?

It was a long and painful meal. She did not remember ever having been so helpless. After she finished, the nurse lowered her bed and left her to rest. Even as simple a thing as eating had been a major crisis. She almost wished she had died in the accident. Except for Eddie. He needed her.

No, Eddie was her brother. She kept mixing it up. Eddie didn't need her.

But someone did. Someone . . .

She was almost asleep, when her eyes opened suddenly. It was happening again, the alertness. As though something was there.

Where?

In the doorway—a flash of white. A quiet step. Her heart began to thud.

She watched, not knowing why it frightened her. She kept her eyes nearly closed so he would think she was sleeping.

He—whoever it was. He was out there, waiting. She knew it.

Again, a faint rustle. Clothes brushing against the wall. And then white. A sleeve.

He was coming in.

Nearly soundless feet. His face in gauze. A surgical mask. Thin black eyebrows that started in one direction, then angled to another.

She had seen those eyebrows. Where?

She gathered herself, unmindful of her pain and weakness. She lifted her head from the pillow and took a sharp breath. She screamed.

Her mouth would not open. It was held fast with wires, her screams muffled by swollen lips.

The man hesitated. His eyes were dark and pitiless.

She screamed again. Her elbow touched a cord on the bed. She fumbled for the call button.

It might be minutes before they answered. Again and again she screamed. The sound was only a small, hoarse cry.

He watched her. Forever. Standing and watching. The pain began to engulf her.

This is when I die.

Wordless thoughts flashed through her mind. He was going to kill her. She would not be able to stop him.

I don't want to die.

She had to live. For Neal and Paul. *My babies.*

He was gone. The doorway where he had stood was empty. She could not believe it.

There came a swift thump of shoes, and a nurse appeared. It was the same nurse who had helped her with lunch.

"What is it, dear? Do you want something for the pain?"

The pain. It was drowning her.

She lifted her hand and pointed toward the door.

"You want the door closed?"

She pointed with short, jabbing motions. No one was there. No one anywhere near the door. She gave up and sank back, surrendering to agony.

"The doctor said you could have medication for the pain," the nurse told her. "I'll be back in a minute."

Don't leave me alone.

She did not want drugs. She must not relax or sleep. But she had no strength to fight when the nurse returned.

Afterward she lay still, waiting for the pain to leave her. Or for something to happen. Perhaps this was only a trick, another way of killing her.

She thought of her young sons. Were they real? Did they exist?

Or was it all part of the dream she had built up, her imagined life with Owen?

2

Owen. She had known him forever. For as long as she had been alive, or so it seemed.

But that couldn't be true. There must have been a time when he did not exist for her. It was probably long ago, for he was a firmly entrenched part of her life. She felt it, although she was not entirely certain of his role.

Yet there must have been a time . . .

A leggy nineteen-year-old with soft brown eyes, filling out a job application form.

GARRITY, Lynette, she wrote, and then her address in Elmhurst, New York, in the borough of Queens.

Elmhurst was noted for its two large gas tanks that made a convenient landmark for traffic reporters: "On the Long Island Expressway, traffic into the city is bumper-to-bumper from the Elmhurst gas tanks."

They had said it just that morning. Her brother Eddie had remarked, "At least it gets us on the map. They don't talk about anybody else's gas tanks."

Eddie, at fourteen, was preoccupied with thoughts of fame and his own plans for achieving it, as either a rock guitarist or a basketball player. Or maybe both. Lynette was more realistic. All she wanted, and which she could reasonably hope for, was a new job with pleasant surroundings. She hated the insurance company where she had worked for a year. She hated its size, its regimentation, the time clock, and the bell that rang at nine and at five, at coffee breaks and lunch hour, just like a school.

Her mother said she was crazy to leave. "It's a big outfit. You have a good chance of meeting somebody."

Which showed how little her mother knew. In a whole year, Lyn had not met anybody who wasn't married, creepy, or gay. Besides, none of her friends had ever married anyone they met in an office. They ended up with boys from the neighborhood, or boys they had known in high school, or met through friends. Lyn still had a supply of such acquaintances, although it was dwindling fast, with many going off to Vietnam and others marrying girls who were, perhaps, more eager than she was.

Meanwhile, she wanted a job that would not depress her. And here, a small real estate office, "conv. to subway," had advertised for a secretary. "Typing & telephone, self-starter." That meant she would be left alone to handle things herself. It sounded pretty good. And "convenient to subway" would be a blessing. It was enough of a hassle getting into the city every morning and out to Elmhurst at night, without having to walk a thousand miles or make an extra connection.

Besides, it seemed a pleasant place. As she filled out her application, she looked around at the office. It was intimate and sunny, and high above Lexington Avenue. A row of potted plants adorned the windowsill. That was another thing about huge companies: you rarely saw a window.

There were only two other women. One was small and gray-haired, the other young and dark, with a diamond ring on her finger.

"Is there just one boss?" Lyn asked the dark-haired girl, who looked up with a smile and took her application.

"Two," was the reply. "Mr. Holdridge and Mr. Tannen."

Mr. Holdridge was out of the office that morning. It would be Mr. Tannen who would see her. After he had had a few minutes to examine her application, she was ushered into his office.

She found herself in another sun-filled room. It contained two massive desks, only one of which was occupied at the moment. Its occupant stood up to shake her hand. He was short and potbellied, with bushy, grizzled eyebrows and the smile of a kewpie doll.

Her mother would have said, "I told you. You shoulda stayed at the insurance company." Lyn took the offered hand. This was what she had wanted, a small place with nice people, where she could have variety in her work.

"And what brings you here?" Mr. Tannen asked cheerfully. "Our ad in the *Times*? Why do you think you want to work for us?"

"Well, uh—" She had not expected such a direct question. "Right now I'm with a big insurance company, and I feel like a piece of machinery. I thought a small place might be more human. And I like it being near the subway."

He looked at her application. "Queens, huh? Yes, you can get right on the Flushing line."

He asked about her typing and shorthand, then said, "Actually, speed isn't all that important here. We don't have a lot of typing, just miserable little things like bills and letters. How are you at working on your own?"

"Oh, I can do that. I like to work that way. That was the main thing in your ad, the self-starter."

The ad had not mentioned salary. He asked what she was earning at the insurance company, then named a figure that was ten dollars a week more. Hardly as generous as she would have liked, but he promised a raise after three months. He shook her hand again and told her to expect a call in a day or so.

As she left his office, Henry Tannen sat contemplating the door that closed behind her. She was probably the best applicant yet. Personable, neatly dressed, and from all appearances, reasonably intelligent.

An attractive girl, no doubt about that. Curvy and long-legged, with a rounded, doll-like face. Not particularly distinguished. No real class, but respectable enough, he supposed. A nice, middle-class girl from one of those millions of row houses in Queens.

Again he perused her application. Nineteen years old. Single. High school education. One year with that incompatible insurance company.

Not much else she could have said about herself. Too young to have done an awful lot. Seemed a little vapid, although presumably she had a life of her own—boyfriends, hopes and dreams, if no real ambition—but it didn't show on the application and it didn't show in her face. Not that it mattered anyway, as long as she was competent, could type and use some initiative.

He ripped a page from his memo pad and scrawled a note to Owen Holdridge.

Typing O.K. I think she'll do.
Rather young, but enthusiastic. Likes "self-starter" idea.
P.S. Nice-looking.

He clipped the note to the girl's application and left it on Owen's desk.

3

Two Mondays later, she began her new job. She arrived at five minutes to nine and found the office door locked. Through its pebbled glass panel she could see gray darkness.

While waiting for someone to come and let her in, she watched other small offices spring to life, watched people step off the elevators with brown paper bags smelling of coffee and cardboard. Each time an elevator opened, she looked for either of the two women, or for Mr. Tannen. The man who finally arrived was one she had not seen before.

He was tall and well built, with a dark, thin face. His nose was aquiline, his eyes cold and green. A gust of September wind had tousled his hair. He combed it with his fingers as he walked toward the door and inserted a key into the lock.

Only then did he notice Lyn.

"Are you the new girl?" He sounded gruff.

"Yes. Lyn Garrity."

He opened the door and turned on a light. She saw that another desk had been set up next to the window. It had its own telephone and a typing ell with a covered typewriter.

"That'll be your place over there," he said. "Which means you have a built-in responsibility for watering the plants." With that, his gruffness vanished. He almost smiled. A dimple-like crease appeared in each cheek.

"Oh, that's fine," she exclaimed. "I like plants."

It was an instantaneous decision. What she really liked was

his face, but her admiration would carry over to the rest of the office.

He showed her where to hang her jacket, then disappeared into the other room, which he shared with Mr. Tannen.

At nine-fifteen, the dark-haired girl with the diamond ring came in. "Hi! I remember your face but not your name. I'm Jackie Fanelli."

The older woman was Doris Peltzer. She arrived late and grumpy, after her subway train had been stalled for an hour in its tunnel under the East River.

These two, Lyn realized, were to be her sole companions. She wondered if she had been right in taking a job with such a small office. It could be either a family or a dead end.

As the days passed, she came to know them well. Jackie lived with her parents in the Bronx and was engaged to a policeman named Mike. Doris was unmarried and shared an apartment in Brooklyn with her widowed sister. Doris's life was the office. She was fiercely possessive of it and of her two employers. It was a kind of surrogate marriage, polyandrous but one-sided. Both men had families of their own. Tannen was a grandfather, and Holdridge kept pictures of his children on his desk.

They were attractive youngsters, the Holdridge boy and girl. Lyn had ample time to admire them that first week when her conferences with their father were interrupted by telephone calls.

"What are their names?" she asked after one lengthy conversation.

He tilted back the twin frames, smiling fondly.

"This is Tina. She's eleven. Just starting to get difficult. Dennis is seven."

It was Friday morning, the last day of her first week at T & H Realty. He had called her in to discuss the current batch of correspondence, but with the mention of his children, they digressed to personal matters.

She learned that he lived in Great Harbor, on the north shore of Long Island.

"That must be a wonderful place for kids," she said, "growing up by the water like that, and all those beaches. Are you near a beach?"

"Not much more than you are, in Elmhurst," he replied. "It's a boat harbor. We usually go to Jones Beach or Sunken Meadow for swimming."

It was an inconsequential discussion, leading nowhere, not even back to the letters. In fact, the letters seemed to have been forgotten. Idly he straightened the two photographs and the ashtray next to them, then rested his hand on the desk, close to hers. He did not take his eyes off her and did not speak. She grew flustered, and said the first thing that came to her mind.

"You should have a picture of your wife, too. You should have the whole family."

"Not Ruth. She's camera-shy."

He said it curtly, shaking his head in annoyance. It seemed an excessive amount of irritation for such a trivial shortcoming. She wondered if perhaps the problem was more fundamental.

"Oh, well, I can understand that." She laughed lightly, to conceal her embarrassment at having brought up a distasteful subject. I don't like my picture taken, either. It always comes out terrible."

He studied her face, an amused smile playing across his mouth.

"I just don't believe that for one second," he said. "I'll bet you take a beautiful picture."

After she returned to her desk, he sat brooding at his.

This was bound to happen—some young thing coming along and looking at him as if he were God. Not that he *was* God, he didn't mean it was bound to happen that way, but only that he should have been able to anticipate this kind of crown to the dissatisfactions that already existed in his life.

He was thirty-seven years old. In three years he would be forty. After forty, a person was middle-aged, or pretty damn near it. And what did he have to show for such a milestone? He had taken his wife's money, invested it in the business, and it all turned out okay. He made a good income for a man his age. He provided a nice life for the wife and kids: a big house in Great Harbor, two late-model cars, and a sailboat. He'd gotten a kick out of the boat, but after three years, what was there to do with it except want a bigger one?

All that, and it wasn't enough. Maybe it was enough for them, but not for him. He wanted—

Damned if he knew what he wanted. He could think of nothing specific except maybe, dammit, a new life. He'd missed so much, and forty was getting kind of late.

The more he thought about it, the more depressed he felt. What had been in it for him? If he died tomorrow, the hole left by his absence would quickly close over and he would be erased. His family would get the insurance. They could go on living in their house, sailing their boat, driving their cars . . .

Handy stuff, insurance. Come to think of it, maybe there wasn't enough. And what if something happened to Ruth? Probably he ought to insure her, too. After all, while the kids were young, she was just about as irreplaceable as he was.

He heard his buzzer in the other room. He had not realized how concretely he was thinking, until he found he had pressed the button.

She took him by surprise, answering so promptly. It was almost as if the matter were taking care of itself, rushing along without him. He handed her a business card.

"Lyn, would you get this man on the phone? If he's not in, leave a message to call back."

"Certainly." She reached out to take the card from him, and their fingers touched. She kept her eyes cast down. He noticed that she had long, thick lashes. Not too much makeup, either.

He liked that. And he liked the way her soft brown hair waved around her face and trailed over her shoulders.

Why hadn't Ruth ever looked like that? The question piqued him as Lyn went back to her desk to put through the call.

But Ruth never had. He remembered that he had once found her sexy, but she had never been anywhere near as sexy as this girl, even at the age of twenty, when he first knew her. With her short, dark, curly hair and full figure that bordered on dumpiness, she had been exactly the sort of girl you could picture as a mother for your children. Now, at thirty-six, there was definitely something matronly about her, even to the clothes she wore.

A buzzer sounded on his desk. He picked up the phone.

"Mr. Holdridge," said Lyn's voice, breathily sweet, "I have your insurance broker for you."

She spent the rest of the day trying not to think about their conversation of that morning. It was not so much what was said that bothered her, as what was felt. She had felt it, and she knew he did, too.

It doesn't matter, she told herself. It doesn't matter if he does. He's a married man.

He left early that evening, saying good-bye to each of the women, but letting his eyes linger for a moment on Lyn.

Jackie looked up from her file drawer. "Good-night, Mr. Holdridge, have a nice weekend."

"Good-night," echoed Lyn, her face warming. Mercifully, no one seemed to notice. The door closed and she went back to her typewriter, trying to picture his house, and the children running to meet him. And his wife, Ruth.

She was curious about Ruth. She imagined someone well groomed and reserved, probably in tweeds, with ash-blond hair hanging in a limp pageboy. Reserved and probably cold, if the mention of her could cause that tight-lipped shake of the head. Not a real glamour girl, not one who carried on affairs and made him angry, for Ruth was a homey name.

Just cold. A disappointment.

He wants someone to love him.

Hurriedly she typed the rest of the letter, and then another. "What do I do?" she asked Jackie, who was belting herself into a bulky white sweater. "He has to sign these and he's already left."

"You're really conscientious, aren't you? What sort of place did you work in before?" Jackie scribbled Mr. Holdridge's name on the letters and added her own initials.

Lyn packed her letters into their envelopes and mailed them as she walked to the subway with Jackie. She felt let down, perhaps because of his hasty departure. She had looked forward to that last moment, when she would take the letters in for his signature.

Am I such a dog, she asked herself angrily, that I have to think like that? Like Doris?

Jackie was rambling on about her fiancé, Mike, and a crowd of antiwar demonstrators. She paused to inquire, "Do you have a boyfriend?"

"Not anything serious," Lyn replied. "Just different ones."

"Are you seeing anybody tonight?"

"No, tomorrow. A guy named Joe Singleton. We went to school together."

Joe Singleton. He had fascinated her once. She remembered how she had felt when he touched her.

She could still be aroused by him, she supposed, but the main part of her feeling had died. She had not realized it until now.

"Well, enjoy yourself," Jackie told her. They said good-bye at the station. Lyn joined a human waterfall down a flight of stairs and then through tunnels to the platform, where she waited for her train.

She was tired when she finally reached home. The trip exhausted her. She turned the last corner, past a small grocery store, to a row of modest attached houses, each with its own narrow back yard and a concrete walk to the front door.

Her brother Eddie was in back of the house, shooting baskets. She could hear it from the front walk. She saw a light in the kitchen and found her mother at the table, drinking coffee to revive herself after a long day at the bakery.

"Is Dad home?" Lyn asked.

"Probably stopped at a bar." Her mother sounded annoyed.

"If you didn't nag him so much, maybe he'd cut down on the drinking."

"If I don't nag him he drinks anyway, and nagging makes me feel better. How's the new job?"

Lyn kicked off her shoes and sat down at the table. "It's great. It's a nice little office, and I like the people."

Her mother looked dubious. She still maintained that the firm was too small. Lyn ought to be meeting young men and getting married like her sister Beverly. Nineteen years old, going on twenty. It was a shame. Bev had been married straight out of high school.

"So what do you do?" she asked, reaching into the drainer for a second coffee cup. "Do you rent out apartments? Offices?"

"No, it's buying and selling. They buy these buildings and hold them for a while, maybe fix them up, and then they sell them. That's where they make their money."

"Whole buildings?"

"Well, they're mostly kind of slums. And lofts. There's a lot of money in lofts. People are fixing them up and living in them."

Her mother sniffed. The economics of real estate were beyond her. She was eager to get to the part that really mattered. "No men, right?"

"What's the hurry?" Lyn demanded. "Your other daughter got married, didn't she? You have your grandchildren."

"Don't get fresh with me. It's you I'm worried about. You

shoulda studied nursing. Then you could go to Veet Nam, where they all are. I bet those girls don't come back single."

"Mom, that's not what they go there for."

"Oh, sure. They only want to serve their country. You got a date this weekend?"

"Yes. Joe Singleton."

"He's a nice boy."

Lyn sighed. "I guess so."

"You guess so. I know so. Where are you going?"

"What?"

"You're not listening. You and Joe. Are you going anywhere special?"

"Bowling, I guess."

"You don't look too happy about it. What did you do, have a fight or something?"

"No, Mom, it's okay. I was just—thinking about something else."

4

She lay in the hospital bed, her own aches and bruises receding as she thought of Owen. Why wouldn't they tell her what had happened to him? It must have been bad, if they wouldn't tell her.

Or maybe they didn't know she cared. Had he been with her in the car? Had he been with her at all, ever, or was he even now married to Ruth?

Outside, she could see that it was still daylight, still the whitish-blue sky. That was all she knew. What month was this? What year? She felt as though some time had gone by since she first met Owen and fell in love. She thought they had been together and shared a life, and that some of his children were hers, but maybe it was only a dream. Maybe the children were part of the dream, the twin boys, Neal and Paul.

Yet she seemed to remember Ruth's children as grown up. The girl Tina, who hated her—and still did, with a hatred that was all the more formidable for being adult.

But maybe that, too, was a dream, a projection of her fear of Tina. It must have been, for she was in a hospital, and the accident had happened right after she went to live in the big house on the hill. Her car had skidded on that hill when the road was icy. She remembered it now.

And Tina—Tina would come and wish her dead. She knew it as surely as if it had already happened.

Tina, the little girl in the portrait on his desk. A pretty little girl with short, curly hair and a pixie face.

Was that where she had seen Tina? In the photograph? She could not distinguish between what had actually happened and what she only fantasized.

Suddenly she was alert again. Footsteps approached her room, slowly, tentatively. She held herself ready to scream.

But the man who appeared in the doorway was Owen.

She gave a little cry. At the sound of it he stopped, and then came toward her, smiling.

She was surprised that he seemed older. Was he really older, or was it from worry over what had happened to her? His hair was grayer than she remembered it, and the creases in his cheeks were deeper.

"I couldn't get here any sooner," he said. "The damned trains . . ."

She reached out to him and made another small sound, trying to say his name.

"You can't talk?" he asked.

Again the negative gesture with her hand.

He pulled over a chair and sat down beside her, crossing his legs.

"That was a pretty bad one this time."

This time. So this was another time, and not the accident on the hill. Or was that not what he meant?

He was sitting at her right side. She could not take his hand, and she wanted to hold it. She wished he would realize that and move to the other side of the bed.

She wished she could talk to him. There was so much she wanted to know.

He said, "I'm sorry, angel. I've given you a lot of trouble. It's been rough, I realize that, but it's over now. I didn't tell you, did I?"

She watched him, waiting to hear more. All he did was pat her arm, the right one, with all its bandages.

Someday, she thought, I'll be able to talk. If I live that long.

He told her he had ordered flowers, and was surprised that they had not yet come. He had ordered them by phone before he left the office. At least he had remembered to do that much, he said, after the terrible news of her accident. She could not begin to imagine how he had felt when he got the phone call from Leigh Elliott.

The name sounded familiar. Leigh Elliott. She frowned, trying to remember.

Leigh Elliott had been driving by, he said, had started to wave to her, and suddenly saw the car go out of control and over the hill.

"Poor Leigh." He shook his head. "I sent some flowers to her, too. She was pretty shocked by the whole thing. Do you realize, if it hadn't been for her, you could have died? Once the car was down over that hill, there's a good chance it wouldn't be seen from the road."

He sat with her for a while longer, then looked at his watch and told her he had better get home and take care of the children. He would see her tomorrow. Or maybe that evening, if he could get away.

He bent to kiss her face, and then was gone.

And she missed him.

She tried to remember whether he had always looked like that. She didn't think so.

But he had talked about the office. Was it the same one where she had met him?

How long ago?

She remembered going back to work that Monday, the second week on her new job. Now there was no longer any mistaking the way he felt about her. Whether she was in his office receiving instructions, or he was passing by her desk, he always seemed to be watching her. His eyes were soft and warm and full of longing.

She liked it, but it frightened her. He was a married man. She had thought she would only daydream about him, and make her life more interesting. But if the attraction was mutual, that could mean trouble.

A week went by. The only times they talked were when she sat beside his desk to discuss their work. Sometimes he asked about her family, or herself. He asked her what she did on weekends.

"I go bowling," she answered, "with friends. Or I shop, or go to the movies. Not very exciting, is it?"

He made her feel very young. He also made her feel special. No one had ever done that before.

He said, "It sounds as if you're waiting for something."

They both looked up, hearing voices in the outer office. The door opened and Mr. Tannen came in. The two men talked over her head about a building on Spring Street. Mr. Holdridge nodded a dismissal to her. She took the work he had given her and went back to her own desk. She felt happy and, at the same time, still apprehensive. She wondered what he would have gone on to say if Mr. Tannen had not come in.

She found out the following Wednesday. It was her third week at T & H Realty.

She was waiting for an elevator on her way to lunch. The office door opened and Mr. Holdridge came out.

"Kind of slow, isn't it?" He nodded toward the elevators. "I always thought they should have an express for the higher floors."

The elevator arrived and they squeezed themselves into a packed cube of humanity.

"Where do you usually eat?" he asked.

"Oh, Chock Full O' Nuts, or someplace."

"Just enough to sustain you. How about having lunch with me?"

She knew her face must have reddened. She was glad when they reached the lobby and she could step off the elevator ahead of him.

"That would be nice." The blush was subsiding. It never would have happened if he had not taken her by surprise.

He steered her toward Third Avenue, to a restaurant called Ricci's. It was dimly lit, uncrowded, and decorated with mural scenes of Venice.

"Would you care for a drink?" he asked when they were seated.

"Only if you're having one."

He ordered scotch on the rocks and she a vodka and tonic. The waiter set a basket of rolls on the table. She buttered one, but did not feel like eating. It was a strange experience, having lunch with her boss, and at the same time, being so aware of his maleness. She did not know what to say to him.

"Did you always live on Long Island?" she asked.

"Pretty much, if you count Brooklyn. That's where I grew up. Ruth did, too. We met at college there."

"You must have been young when you got married."

"It was a while after that. And then a few more years before we had kids."

She imagined those years when he and Ruth had been newlyweds, keeping house together. She wished she had known him when he was younger.

He took a gold cigarette case from his breast pocket. "Do you smoke?"

"Yes, thank you."

He lit her cigarette with a lighter that matched the case.

"How about you?" he asked. "You told me about your bowling dates. Anybody serious?"

"Not really. Just guys I knew in school, and they're kind of boring."

"What's your idea of interesting?"

"Oh, I don't know." She watched the smoke curl from her cigarette. "I like a man who's been around for a while and gotten some depth. I think older men are politer, too."

He chuckled. "Maybe we try harder."

She had wanted only an entrée. He urged her to take the works—appetizer, dessert, and a refill of coffee. Lunch drifted into its second hour. They smoked cigarette after cigarette while they talked.

"When you finished school," he said, adding sugar to his third cup of coffee, "what did you see ahead for yourself? You must have had some idea of how you wanted your life to go."

"I planned to work for a while and then get married."

"And you're right on target."

"Not with the second part of it. I told you they're all abysmal."

"I can't believe a lovely girl like you would waste her time on abysmal people. Tell me about them."

He couldn't really be interested. She wondered why he asked.

"Well, there's Joe Singleton. He drives a taxi days and goes to school at night."

"What's wrong with that?"

She shrugged, admitting to herself that she was not being fair. It was no mean feat on Joe's part to push himself through night school after a hard day of cab-driving.

"Maybe," she said, "he'll improve with age."

He finished his coffee and paid the check. As they walked back to the office, he put his arm around her waist. She looked up at the bright September sky, feeling something leap inside her. She would never forget his touch.

Later, sitting at his desk, he listened to the sound of her typewriter and remembered how she had felt when he put his arm around her. A sudden stiffening, as though in surprise, and then a kind of melting.

She felt something for him, no doubt about it. She talked about that Singleton fellow and the others, and how "boyish" they were. He supposed his maturity must have been a powerful attraction, but that couldn't be the only thing. After all, thirty-seven wasn't so old, and he looked much younger.

He might seem old to her. What was she, nineteen? He was just a year short of being twice her age.

But the gap would shrink in time. Next year he would be two years short of twice her age. Anyhow, it wasn't so important, as long as they could talk to each other. They got along fine, much better than he did with Ruth, a fact of which Ruth, poor girl, seemed totally unaware. From the depths of her domestic activities, she failed to notice any change in their relationship.

But there was a big change. He had to face it: she didn't attract him any more, and it was her own fault. She had stopped being his wife and turned into a mother. Nothing but a mother. A man had the right to something more than that.

5

I love him, she thought as she felt herself waking. *I love him.*

Her eyes opened into darkness. But the darkness was incomplete. As she turned her head and saw light spilling through the partly closed door, she remembered that she was not at home in Elmhurst, dreaming of Owen. She was in a hospital.

She tried to move her hand, to reach for the place in her chest where it hurt, and found her fingers clumsy with bandages. She had forgotten.

The blind above her bed was still open. Through its slats she could see a star twinkling.

Crepe-soled feet padded down the corridor past her door. In the distance, a telephone rang with a muted beep and voices floated from the nurses' station. A hospital was like a little city that only slowed at night, but did not sleep.

I love him.

She thought he loved her, too. He never said so, at least not right away.

It happened later. Instead of love, he told her he wanted her. Was it the same?

It was the week following their lunch in the restaurant. She had worked late to finish some photocopying, which took a long time because the copier broke down and she had to wait for a repairman. For once, Owen had not run out to catch his train. After a while, they were the only two remaining in the office.

When she finally finished, he was ready to leave, too. He locked and bolted the door and set the burglar alarm.

"Are you in a hurry to get home," he asked, "or would you like to stop somewhere and have a drink?"

"I'd love it." She wondered if she ought to call home. She could scarcely tell them she was going out with her married boss.

They walked through Grand Central Station and crossed Vanderbilt Avenue to the Biltmore Hotel. She saw him look about nervously as they entered the cocktail lounge. Something folded inside her, and for a moment, she felt cheap. Then he turned to her, all graciousness, led her to a corner table and helped her off with her jacket.

"What will you have?" he asked. "Another vodka and tonic?"

"I guess so."

A question nagged her: Where was all this leading? What was she to him?

She looked at him, wanting to ask. All she could think of was a very oblique probe.

"You'll miss your train."

He grinned, showing the creases in his cheeks. "There are always others."

"Do you ever wish you lived in the city? It would be a lot easier, wouldn't it?"

"It would be, in many ways."

"But I suppose the country's better for your wife and kids."
Please say something about Ruth. Anything. Tell me about her.

"For the kids, anyway," was all he said.

Their drinks arrived. She poked with her stirrer at the wedge of lime floating in hers, trying to squeeze out some of its juice.

"Would your wife rather live in the city?"

"My wife," he replied, flicking on his cigarette lighter and studying the flame, "wants whatever is good for the kids. I would say that's probably her most outstanding characteristic."

"What?" she asked, bewildered.

"Hovering. It's a little hard to explain in so many words, but it makes for a deteriorating situation." He snapped the lighter closed and dropped it into his pocket.

"I suppose I had a lot to do with it," he went on. "She had the children and I had the business. Both were growing and needed attention. That didn't leave either of us with much time or energy for—each other."

"Oh . . ."

"And so we kept going in different directions." He stared into his drink.

She waited for some elaboration. Finally she said, "But you're still together."

"Ostensibly. For the children. But that's about it."

Now she knew what he was trying to tell her. The only thing she could not be sure of was what she felt about it. Dread? Outrage? Excitement? Or all of them?

She asked, thinking of its effect upon the children, "Do you fight with her a lot?"

"We coexist."

"Maybe that's worse, I don't know. My parents fight. I think, if people don't get along, they shouldn't stay together just for the children. It's too much tension in the air. Children always know."

He looked at her as though seeing something new. "Is that right?"

"Well, that's what I think. It's really none of my business. I should keep quiet."

"Why? It's a free country." He reached across the table and took her hand. "Beautiful Lynette. Where did you ever get a name like Lynette? It's so frilly."

"My godmother. Sometimes I think they did it on purpose, to make up for wishing I was a boy."

"I'm glad you're not. I like things the way they are. Except—" The fingers tightened on hers. "I'd like to know you better. Much better, Lynette."

A drink here, dinner there, and sometimes lunch, when he was not busy making his rounds of properties, lawyers, prospective buyers and sellers. Autumn turned into winter. A snowfall left soot-encrusted ice underfoot. It soon disappeared from the midtown area, but remained grimy and treacherous in Elmhurst until a night of rain washed it away.

On Christmas Eve, the office closed at one o'clock. She remained at her desk, typing the letters he had dictated that morning. She knew he was still there, although the others had left. Her body was tense with anticipation—but of what, she did not know. He would have to leave soon, get on a train and go home to his children.

She wondered how it would be, waking up at his house on Christmas morning. She tried to imagine the house, and saw carpets everywhere. A carpet on a majestic stairway that curved down into the living room, with a Christmas tree in the niche at its foot.

A carpet on the bedroom floor. Brown, with light blue drapes. She had no idea what the house was really like. She saw them asleep in a double bed, their backs to each other. Or would they have twin beds? She saw the children bursting in to wake them. Whatever was wrong between Ruth and himself, at least that day would be for the children. They would be happy. All of them.

She gazed out of the window at the lights in the building across the street. It was a dark, cloudy afternoon. Jackie had talked tritely of a white Christmas, although it would probably rain instead of snow.

She heard a file drawer close in the inner office. Then he stood at the doorway, a frown between his eyes.

"What's all this? Why aren't you on your way home?"

His voice had an odd lilt. He had known she would not be on her way home.

"Just finishing up the letters," she explained. It was like reading lines that had already been written, as though they had to pretend, even to the empty office.

Fifteen minutes later she typed the last set of initials and took the letters to him for his signature.

"Sit down," he said, gesturing toward the chair beside his desk. He read through the letters, scrawled his name, folded them and stuffed them into their envelopes. Then he looked up at her.

"Merry Christmas, Lyn."

Before she could respond, he took her in his arms. There had been quick kisses before, but nothing like this. They had never found a time or a place. She could feel his tongue pushing its way into her mouth, his hand working the flesh on her back and then moving to cup her breast through the soft blue sweater.

He murmured something. She thought it was her name. He drew away and said, "This is a hell of a place."

Place for what? She was suddenly afraid, and at the same time, excited.

He kissed her again. Then he stood her up as though she were a doll.

"I have something for you."

He opened his desk drawer and took out a small white package tied with a gold ribbon.

"But I don't have anything for you," she said.

"I don't need anything, darling. This was just something I wanted to do. Why don't you open it?"

"It's so beautifully wrapped . . ." She pulled at an end of the ribbon. Inside the paper was a black plush jeweler's box.

"You shouldn't—" she began.

"Don't tell me I shouldn't. I make these decisions for myself."

It was not a reproach. His voice was kind and caressing.

She opened the box. In a bed of white satin lay a gold, heart-shaped pendant on a fine gold chain. The center of the heart was a rectangular green stone.

"That's an emerald," he said into the silence.

She gasped the first words that came to her. "A *real* one?" It sounded terrible. Greedy and shallow. She hadn't meant it that way.

He laughed. "A real one. I hope you like it."

"I didn't mean—I just meant—You shouldn't have. Really. You shouldn't do this."

Still clutching the box, she put her arms around his neck. As they kissed, she felt herself beginning to yield. This might be the time. She had never let anyone make love to her before.

His hand reached under her sweater. She flinched in alarm, then again melted toward him.

Suddenly he pulled away. "This is ridiculous."

She straightened her sweater and skirt, and could not look at him.

"You're half afraid, aren't you?" he asked. She nodded.

He said, "You shouldn't be. It's me. Owen. You're not a virgin, are you?"

"Yes, I am."

"Good God, you make me feel like a dirty old man."

"Well, I can't help being a virgin. I mean, I can't help it right now."

He kissed her again lightly, and said, "In that case, I'm glad we couldn't—that these aren't the best of conditions. I don't want to be the one to take a young girl's innocence."

"That's not the only thing."

"What else is there?"

"You're married."

He stared at her in brief surprise, and then smiled.

"But, Lyn, that's separate. It's way out on Long Island. It's—"

"I knew you'd say that. I don't know why, but men always seem to think that way, and women just don't."

"I do love you, you know." He reached for her again, gently, not insisting. They stood wrapped in each other's arms.

"Do you know I love you?" he persisted, giving her a final kiss on the forehead.

"I guess so. At least I do now."

"Why don't you put on the necklace? I want to see you wear it."

She opened the box and lifted out the pendant. It would hardly be enhanced by her blue sweater, but she couldn't tell him that. He helped her fasten it, then kissed the back of her neck. When she turned around, he studied her face and not the jewel.

"I wanted something to match you," he said, sitting in his desk chair and pulling her onto his lap. "I thought this went with your personality. Couldn't get anything to match your eyes. The only brown stones are semiprecious, and that wasn't good enough."

"You're sweet to say that." Her fingers crawled up his necktie and touched his chin. "But you have green eyes. Somebody should give you an emerald. Do you know, when I first saw you, I was afraid of you. I thought your eyes looked cold."

"Really? Are you afraid of me now?"

"Of course not. You're a child. That's probably why Ruth likes you."

His mouth compressed in a wry smile. She remembered the first time the subject of Ruth had come up between them.

There was definitely a little fire to go with the smoke, she decided, scarcely aware that he was watching her. Maybe Ruth felt it, too. Maybe she would be the one to initiate a breakup.

"Did I say something?" Lyn asked.

He patted her thigh. "You're a perceptive little girl. Don't overdo it."

He thought about that conversation later, on the train going home. He had hated to leave her on the subway, that depressing sardine can, although he had ridden with her to

Woodside and caught his own train from there. He could do
that much for her—keep her company.

He remembered what she had said about Ruth's liking him
because he was a child. He certainly was not a child, but he
felt she had hit some kind of nail on the head, even without
knowing Ruth.

What was it, exactly? Not a mothering so much as a managing. Maybe not even that. It was just that she classified him
together with the children as her "family." Meaning her
charges and responsibilities. Rather, she was *his* responsibility,
but she failed to see it that way. When she prepared his dinner
and did all the things she was supposed to do as homemaker,
she did it with the air that he could not do those things for
himself. A kind of fond, amused condescension that was really
out of place.

He dozed, thinking of Lyn and her soft body under that
sweater. He wished there were some way that he could be
with her. It seemed cheap to take her to a hotel. And it would
be her first time, too, if what she said was true. There should
be nothing cheap about it.

At last the train reached Great Harbor. He stepped off
among people carrying parcels and shopping bags. Thank God
Ruth took care of all that for the family. He recollected that he
didn't have anything for her, but then, he never knew what to
give her. He usually handed her an envelope of cash, crisp new
bills, and told her to buy something for herself. That way she
could get what she really wanted. It kept them both happy.
The only thing was, in shopping for Lyn, he had forgotten to
ask the bank for crisp new bills. He would have to give Ruth
old ones, and there weren't as many as there should have been,
but what did it really matter? It was still money.

Ruth met him at the door after she heard Dennis screeching,
"It's Daddy! Daddy!"

She looked briefly to see whether he was carrying anything,
but he wasn't, except his usual black portfolio. It would be

cash again. To buy whatever she wanted. And she couldn't think of anything she wanted, except a surprise. From him.

She wished he would buy something for the children, too. Just a small anything, it didn't matter, as long as he partici- pated. But like most men, he simply couldn't think when it came to gifts. Helplessly, he turned the whole job over to her.

"Merry Christmas, darling." She put her hand around his cold neck and kissed his cold face. "You didn't have the heater on in your car."

"Just to drive from the station?" He tousled Dennis's hair and patted Tina's cheek. He seemed worried about something. She hoped it was not another lawsuit, or anything serious.

"It's just that you felt cold, that's all." She knew she was talking trivia, but did not want to ask about a lawsuit in front of the children. "Do you think it's going to rain or snow?"

"It's going to snow!" yelped Dennis.

"I hope so, precious." She bent down to hug him. He started to pull away, but thought better of it and allowed her the hug. He was still her little boy. At least she had someone. Tina was growing up, and as for Owen, there were times when she felt that she had lost him somewhere.

6

Lyn had never been lonely at Christmas before. That year she was glad when it was over. It had seemed as though her family and friends were strangers, or at best, irrelevant.

Winter began in earnest, with cold winds, ice, and slush. She wore boots to the office and he commented on how cute she looked in them. He took her to dinner that night, but it did not end with dinner. Their relationship was rolling ahead inexorably, picking up speed. She knew what would happen. And it did, although not in the elegant Commodore Hotel, where she had imagined it, but in a modest hostelry farther down on Lexington Avenue.

It seemed so inevitable when it happened. She no longer minded that they were not married, or that he was married to someone else. She was carried along as though in a dream.

After that they visited the hotel sometimes once a week, sometimes less often. He talked longingly of setting up an apartment, if he could find the right place. She wondered how "right" it had to be. Anything would have been better than this fly-by-night arrangement and the hotel clerk who nodded knowingly when they gave their fictitious names.

January turned into February, and then it was March. The office threw a party for Jackie, who would soon be getting married. Lyn envied her, and reflected with a pang on her own hopeless situation.

But it couldn't be hopeless. No one would go on forever

staying married to a woman he did not love, and who did not love him. They could only be punishing themselves—and for what?

But maybe Ruth didn't know.

"Does Ruth know about us?" she asked one evening. It was Friday, and they were at Ricci's, just finishing their dinner. Unless they rented a room at the hotel, they could meet only in public places like this, for there was no other place.

"Of course not," he answered. "There'd be hell to pay. Do you want problems?"

"How do you explain it to her when you don't go home for dinner?"

"Office work. What else? But I'm covered even if she calls, because a lot of work doesn't take place in the office."

The waiter brought their coffee and hovered about, dabbing up a spill on a saucer, bringing a pitcher of cream. He knew them by now. Several of the waiters did.

"Would it be so awful if she found out? You said there wasn't anything—It seems to me, with all these late nights, she ought to be able to guess."

He was silent for a moment. Then he said, "I don't know what I'd do without Ruth."

She felt her face drain. He was intent upon his coffee, moving the cup in circles and watching the liquid form an inverted cone.

"She's a wonderful, wonderful woman," he went on. "The very best. I don't know what I ever did to deserve such luck. But there's always—I don't know."

"What don't you know?"

He set down the cup and regarded her with a teasing half smile. "You should wear that more often. It's very becoming."

She looked down to see what she was wearing. A knit dress of mulberry red. Yes, she did look nice in it, but all she could think of was the contrast in his manner. Serious and heartfelt for Ruth, playful for her.

That's all I am, she thought. Just a playmate.

"Shall we go?" he asked. "I can give you a lift home."

He had driven his car into the city instead of taking the train. Parking in a midtown garage was expensive, but he had done it several times, so that she would not have to go home on the subway late at night. It was not really late, only nine o'clock, but she had a five-block walk from the station to her house, and it worried him.

"It's very nice of you," she said as he helped her on with her coat. "Do you know what I like about you? You're so thoughtful. Even little things like coats. And none of the other guys I know would go to so much trouble to drive me home."

"Other guys? Do you still date other guys?"

"Well, sure. I have to do something with my weekends."

He held her arm and they walked in silence through a mild night to the garage. She wondered if she had made him angry.

"They don't mean very much," she said.

"Then why do you do it?"

"Well, because—I love you, Owen, and I can't see loving anybody else, but—"

"But what?"

"I can't help wondering, is this supposed to be my life?"

He gave her a quick, sidelong glance, his face sober and full of questions, but he said nothing. They reached the garage and she waited while he paid for his parking. She thought the conversation was at an end, but after they were in the car and he had negotiated the sharp corner out of the garage, he asked, "What do you mean 'is this supposed to be your life'?"

"I mean, it's not really going anywhere, is it?"

"Where do you want it to go?"

She closed her eyes. "I can't see spending my life just being somebody's girlfriend. It's not really a life that way. And what I want, I can't have with you, because there's Ruth, and you said you love her."

"When did I say I love her?"

She caught her breath. "Back there at the restaurant. You said you didn't know what you'd do without her."

"That's true, I don't. But think about it, darling. Is that necessarily love?"

He turned east on Fifty-eighth Street, crossed Second Avenue and drove up the ramp to the Queensboro Bridge. Their tires hummed on the exposed metal grid. She looked down the East River and back at the bright lights of Manhattan.

"Even if you don't love her," she said, "you're still married to her. You have your family with her, and it ends up the same for me whether you love her or not."

He smiled faintly as they wound down the long ramp on the Queens side of the bridge.

"So you're keeping your options open," he said.

"What do you mean?"

"By seeing other men. That's what started us on this topic, if I remember correctly."

"It's more than just a topic. It's very important to me."

"What is?"

Down Van Dam Street, past factories and warehouses, and up another ramp to the Long Island Expressway. She knew the way perfectly by now.

"My future." Why couldn't he understand?

"Yes, I can see that. I suppose I was thinking more of the present than the future."

"You already have your future."

"In a way. But I don't think anybody really feels that he has, even when it looks as if things are settled. Most of us start asking the same question you're asking: 'Is this all there's ever going to be?'"

She thought of her own parents, and knew it was true. It surprised her that even Owen, with his advantages, did the same thing.

"So what are you saying?" she asked. "Are you saying you might—that you and Ruth—"

"I'm saying nothing's permanent. Nothing should be considered permanent."

They were on the expressway, merging, crossing lanes. The traffic was heavy even at this time of night.

"Do you mean you'd really ask her for a divorce?"

"I've thought about it."

"What about the children?"

"You said yourself it isn't always good for the children to have parents who don't get along, and I agree."

"But just tonight you told me you were so lucky to have her."

"I am."

"I don't think I understand you."

He reached over and massaged her thigh. "I don't understand me, either. All I know is that Ruth is a fine woman and I've always admired her, but you're the one I love. If you think you're confused about all this and don't know what to do with yourself, just remember, you've got company."

She had to be content with that. It was nothing but a declaration of love, and not a very romantic one, but she understood that it was all he could give her for the moment.

He did not walk her to the door when they reached her house. The last time he had done it, her father came out to see who was with her. She had managed to gloss over the introductions and explain nothing, but it had been awkward.

Half an hour later she lay in bed, feeling the early spring night around her. It was deliciously mild, almost like May instead of March.

She wondered what he would say to Ruth. She wished she could be completely happy, but she was not. It meant the breaking up of a family. And yet the family, according to him, already showed fracture lines. She had not been the cause of that.

She woke to the *thunk* of her brother's basketball against the side of the house.

It was Saturday. Two whole days before she would see

Owen again. She tried to recapture her thoughts of last night. The optimism was no longer there.

She remembered how he had talked of Ruth. She had to face it, those words had come from his heart.

Probably he was the kind of man who would always try for a conquest. Maybe he really thought it was love, but in the end he would want and need Ruth.

Discouragement weighed heavily as she got out of bed. It was lightened only by self-respect and a new resolution. Her course would not be easy, but as long as she recognized the truth, she might be able to stay on top of the situation instead of under it.

I love him, she told herself deliberately, feeling it seep through her. *But I don't have to love him.*

She could love Joe Singleton instead.

Joe Singleton was attractive in a young, animal way. Part of what she liked about Owen was his maturity. He was complex and civilized, a real person. He had achieved something. A position, perhaps. He was part of the world, with that house in the suburbs, and his family. And maybe that in itself intrigued her—the fact that he was unattainable. Or maybe she only wanted to trade places with Ruth.

As Owen wanted her to.

She had a date that night with Joe. He arrived in his second-hand Impala and parked in front of the house to wait for her. When she went out to join him, her brother Eddie was leaning in the car window, clutching his basketball to his stomach.

Joe peered out at her. "Hey, Lyn, this kid says he's been shooting baskets all day. Why don't they let him on the team?"

"I told you," Eddie said, "they want taller guys. But I'm going to be better than all of them. They'll have to let me on next year."

"Maybe you'll have a growth spurt," Lyn encouraged him. "Good-night, Eddie."

As she got into the car, he turned away and dribbled his ball down the cement walk.

Joe said, "I feel sorry for that kid. He wants it so bad."

"So do I. I love Eddie."

Already Joe was suffering by comparison. Owen would have gotten out of the car and opened the door for her. Joe simply sat there.

"You should," he said. "He's your brother."

"I love him better than anybody else in the family."

She watched Joe drive. He lounged in his seat and steered casually with the fingers of one hand. Owen drove more intently and conventionally. And probably more safely, although Joe had never had an accident.

The street lights glinted on his golden brown hair. He had bright blue eyes, and his nose was thin like Owen's.

She tried to imagine herself loving him. All she could feel at the moment was a physical attraction for his strong young body. He would never be anything like Owen, who was worth a hundred of him.

Joe asked, "Where do you want to go?"

"I don't know. Someplace where we can look at the water."

"What water?"

"Joe, we're on an island. We're surrounded by water."

And Owen was near the same water.

"You mean just go and look at it? What for?"

"Let's drive out to Great Harbor. There are a lot of nice houses."

"You want to look at houses?" Almost imperceptibly, the car increased its speed.

She put out her hand. "Not on Saturday night. Not really. I was kidding."

They ended up at a movie. It was a dramatic story of the Marines in World War II, and it absorbed him. She had expected him to try to make love to her, but all he did was hold her hand and rub it absentmindedly while he whispered excited comments about the film. Afterward they went to a diner for coffee.

"You still want to go to Great Harbor?" he asked.

"No, forget it. It's silly to go all the way out there."

They selected College Point for a view of the water. He parked on a dark street near the shore of the East River, which flowed into Long Island Sound. She thought of the Sound as it must be at Great Harbor, where she imagined a marina filled with yachts, cabin cruisers, and sailboats of all sizes.

Joe put his arm around her and she snuggled against him.

"What did you want to go and look at houses for?" he asked, nuzzling her hair.

"I don't know. I like houses."

"But why out there? I could never afford anything like that."

"It's okay. Who'd want to rattle around in a mansion, anyway? Can you see me cleaning all those bathrooms?"

"You'd have a maid. A whole lot of maids. But not if you marry me."

She stirred, trying to turn so that she could see him, but he held her tightly.

"Marry you, Joe?"

She managed to make it sound breathless and full of excitement. He seemed to hear the wonder in her voice.

"You would?" he asked. "I thought—I didn't think you were ready yet."

"To get married?"

"For me."

She turned to face him. His mouth moved toward hers. She responded with a physical passion. It was all she could feel for him now, but the rest would come later. It would have to happen, because she would force herself to stop loving Owen.

She would survive by thinking only of now, and never seeing all the years ahead.

7

I did marry Joe!

The recollection surprised her. But where was Joe now? The only man she really remembered was Owen.

The window above her bed showed a dull gray light. The sounds in the corridor had increased. Voices spoke louder now that night was gone. Footsteps were brisker and busier.

She had been asleep. Was it all a dream? It felt too real to be a dream, but she could not remember when it happened. Was it yesterday? Or long ago?

She remembered marrying Joe, but what then?

The door moved suddenly. A large blond nurse came into the room and offered her a thermometer.

"Do you think you can manage it? Your mouth is pretty swollen."

She allowed the thermometer to be slipped under her tongue, and held it in place with her hand. The touch stung her. She saw no need to have her temperature taken when she wasn't sick. Only hurt.

Very hurt. It had not always been like this. Once she had been able to move about and talk like a normal person.

She tried to remember the crash. Her face must have hit the steering wheel, if that was possible.

But she had been lying down, looking up at the sky. Or maybe that was only after it started to roll, or after the crash.

She could still feel it sliding down the hill, that horrible sensation of having no control.

I was not driving, she remembered with sudden clarity. *But I was alone in the car.*

The nurse took the thermometer and examined it. "Have a good day, now," she said as she left the room.

The patient closed her eyes, remembering terror. Who had put her there? In the car. Lying down, hurt and helpless, and feeling the car begin to slide.

"Owen," she whimpered, her voice making only a small moan. It was Owen she wanted.

But she had married Joe.

Their wedding was hasty and informal. She expected most people to assume that she was pregnant, and they did. She was only glad they didn't know the truth—that she was escaping from a forbidden love.

Even Owen did not guess. She was married on a Saturday, and on Monday arrived at the office wearing her new wedding ring.

He had not yet come in. She felt let down, and at the same time, relieved. And when she looked up from her work a few minutes later and saw a shadow at the pebbled pane in the door, she snatched off her ring and slipped it into her purse.

Carefully he greeted Doris first, and then Lyn. Jackie, as usual, was late. He went to the inner office and sat down at his desk, out of sight. She heard him opening the mail, dropping pieces of it into the wastebasket, dialing the telephone. And then he summoned her.

His voice was soft. "Lyn?"

Her heart began to pound. She knew she was not cured of him at all.

Without his asking, she closed the door between the two offices. He raised an eyebrow suggestively.

She felt stricken. What had she done? Anything was better

than this, even the old way of never knowing her future. At least then she could still be with him.

"I have something to tell you," she said.

"Yes?" He only half paid attention as he sorted through the rest of the mail.

"I was getting too involved with you, and it wasn't right."

He looked up at her, fully listening now.

"There's this man I know—" Deliberately she added, "About my own age. I've been seeing him almost every weekend. Well, I—we—got married."

"You what?"

"I had to."

He looked shocked. "Why didn't you tell me?"

"No, I don't mean that. I just meant—It was better. For you, too. And I wanted a life of my own."

He stared at her. The surprise, which at first had left his face naked, disappeared. He became guarded.

"Who is this—boy?" The slight hesitation made it sound like a sneer.

"He's a man, not a boy. I told you about him. Joe Singleton."

His lips worked. "Lyn, you didn't have to do this."

She had hurt him almost as badly as she had hurt herself. Perhaps he really loved her after all.

"I think I did." She looked at the door, fearful that Doris might hear them. "I told you, we were getting too involved and going nowhere. It was bad for me, and it wasn't right for you. Or for Ruth."

He said with quiet sarcasm, "I'm glad you're so concerned about Ruth."

"Well—she's your wife."

"That's my problem. You didn't have to do what you did. I wish you hadn't."

"Maybe I did have to. Maybe I wanted to. It's my life, and maybe I want something out of it." She stopped guiltily at the sound of the outside door.

They heard Henry Tannen's voice, and then Jackie's "Oh gee, am I late!"

Owen scowled at his desk. "We'll talk about it later."

She did not know what more there was to say. When he insisted upon taking her out for a drink after work "to celebrate," she thought perhaps he would fire her.

Instead of celebrating, they quarreled. He told her she had been an idiot.

"Why?" she begged, as the vodka loosened her tears. "You just wanted to keep me for your convenience. You want—"

"Why'd you have to throw yourself away on a guy like that?"

"Like what? He's perfectly good. He's not as established as you are, because he's younger."

She had meant to add, "And he has to put himself through college," but she checked it. *Younger* stood by itself. And it cut.

She saw the hurt in his eyes and wanted to reach out to him, but he had asked for this. She saw the longing: Two young people with their lives ahead of them, their dreams still to be dreamed. In the end, they might never have what he and Ruth had, but now, at least, they could hope and plan. As for him, she could see by the bleakness in his face that he was back to his old question: Is this all there's ever going to be?

She left her job and took another in an engineering firm on Forty-third Street. Despite the fact that she was only a few blocks from T & H Realty, there was not much chance of her running into Owen among the thousands of people who worked in midtown Manhattan.

"It's not that I want to quit," she had told him. "I love this job, but I can't be near you."

And she knew from the way he looked at her that she was right. He had not given her up. He, who was unfaithful in his own marriage, did not see why she couldn't be, too, as long as they loved each other.

Joe had found a one-bedroom apartment in a six-story brick building in Elmhurst. It had its own off-street parking area. The neighborhood was old and settled, with full-grown shade trees lining the streets.

"This is real class," he told her, "but it's rent-controlled, and with both of us working . . ."

She loved it, a home of her own. Hers and Joe's.

At last her mother and father were proud of her. She was married and living in a "real nice place." They told her she should have put off the wedding for a while and saved her money to buy good furniture, instead of making do with odds and ends.

"Don't worry, we'll take care of it," she answered. "I'm going to keep working and we'll get the place all furnished before we have kids."

She loved her new life. It was not as arduous as she had expected, working, commuting, and keeping house. On most evenings, Joe's classes prevented him from coming home for dinner, and she did not bother cooking for herself. She cleaned and shopped on Saturday morning while he drove his taxi, and she felt like a real wife. They had their Sundays together, and they had their nights. That was what mattered. Joe was a young man of limitless energy. Even with his heavy schedule, he was ready for her at night.

Lovemaking with Joe was more heated and tempestuous than it had been with Owen. It was physically exciting, but she missed Owen's tenderness. Or maybe she missed Owen.

Night after night she tried to lose herself in Joe, in his passion.

"I love you," she whispered, running her hands over his body, adoring his muscles and the smoothness of his skin.

She could make herself believe that she loved him. It was a physical love. She was part of him, and he of her. He thrilled her in a way that Owen never had.

But thrills were not enough. While she looked forward to the hot and heavy nights, they left her feeling empty.

She had been cheated. It wasn't fair. Other people had the things they wanted. Why couldn't she?

Joe worked for a taxi fleet that had its headquarters in Long Island City. He drove there in his own car, often dropping Lyn at the subway station on his way.

For the latter part of a week in mid-May, Joe was forced to take the subway himself. His car was at a repair shop undergoing a major brake job.

By the time the shop called on Saturday morning to say the car was ready, Joe had left for work. Lyn would have to go and pick it up herself.

She felt a quivering of excitement as she boarded the bus. This would be the first time she had ever had the car, any car, to herself with no questions asked. As soon as she was behind the wheel, she headed toward the Long Island Expressway. She felt nervous about driving on a high-speed thoroughfare with her limited experience, but it was the way *he* traveled. She had studied the map many times, tracing his route, as a way of feeling closer to him. She knew which exit to take and where to go from there. The only thing she was not sure of was the network of small roads in Great Harbor itself. Many of them were not shown on the map.

She drove along Great Harbor's main street. It looked like main streets everywhere. A shoe store, a children's clothing store, a picture-framing shop.

Maybe not everywhere, she decided. In some neighborhoods, people did not have pictures to frame.

She watched the shoppers, wondering if she would see him. She had no idea what he did on Saturday mornings.

As she waited for a traffic light, one of the women crossing the street just in front of her might have been Ruth. She would never know.

She wondered if she would recognize the children from their photographs.

At the next light, she made a right turn. The street became residential, lined with modest houses. Not here, certainly. He had told her he lived at the top of a hill. Long Island did not have many hills, but there were a few, particularly in this area. She drove back and forth, searching for high ground.

The houses grew more imposing and farther apart. Upper middle class, whatever that was. At least she knew his address, if she could find the right road.

Suddenly she saw it. Purdue Lane. It had been difficult, but easier than she expected. She drove along it and discovered from the descending numbers that she was heading the wrong way. She dared not turn in any of the elegant driveways, and proceeded to the next intersection where she drove around a block that seemed to continue for miles. She caught a glimpse of an inlet that was probably part of the Sound. It was bordered with rushes and had a murky odor.

Back to Purdue Lane. She began to discern a slight difference between the houses on Purdue and those nearer the Sound, even that smelly bit of backwater she had seen. At first they had all appeared huge to her, but these were a few degrees smaller and the grounds around them were smaller, too. Hardly more than generous-sized lots.

It was not always easy to see the numbers, for some of the houses were set back from the road. She saw 149 on a mailbox, and knew she must be approaching 157.

It was past the next intersection. The hill was not a high one, but part of it was steep, where it dropped off near a curve in the driveway. And she knew it was the right house. She recognized his car parked in front of it.

She was disappointed that the house was not closer to the road. She wanted to be able to see it clearly, and see any of the family who might be outside.

It was a sprawling white house, all on one level, with the roof slightly raised in the central part of it. She supposed that was the living room. Various wings seemed to go off at right angles to each other. He had mentioned a terrace where they had barbecues. That must have been in the back.

A car passed by, and she drove farther onto the shoulder. She opened her map and spread it on the seat, to give an excuse for being there. When she looked up at the house again, the front door opened. A young boy in a red jacket and brown pants came out and turned to wave to someone in the house.

Dennis. That was Dennis. He was too far away for her to see clearly, but she recognized his hair from the picture on Owen's desk. The boy galloped down the driveway. He seemed to come straight toward her, but soon scrambled over the embankment at the edge of the drive and disappeared into a wooded area.

The house was quiet now. She waited another minute and then drove slowly away.

8

From the kitchen window, Ruth watched her boy run down the driveway, then cut over the hillside toward Mark Prensky's house. When he disappeared into the woods, she went back to the living room where Owen was pouring another whiskey for their guest.

"Owen, there's a car parked on the road at the end of the driveway. A green car, just sitting there. I was worried about Dennie."

"Worried, why?" The distraction made Owen pour too much. He handed the overfull glass to his friend Russ, who skimmed off the top with a loud sucking noise.

"Why would a car just be sitting there?" She did not feel she had his attention. "I don't like some of the things that have been going on around here."

"What things?"

"Oh, you know." But maybe he didn't. He spent most of his waking time in the city.

"All the things we came here to get away from," she explained. "Three houses broken into and a girl attacked at the railroad station. I keep being afraid something might happen to the children."

He was listening to her now. Both men watched her, and she felt uneasy. She did not like Russ. Owen said he was an old friend from high school. They had run into each other again in a bar about two years ago. She was surprised to learn that Russ

Jaeger had gone to high school at all, but maybe that was only prejudice on her part. He struck her as something of a punk, with his florid face, bull neck, and Brooklyn accent sprinkled with obscenities.

He had mentioned a wife. She wondered why he had not brought his wife when he came all the way out to Great Harbor for a visit. She would have liked it better with another woman there. He had been startled when she asked, then quickly replied that his wife had gone to visit her mother, who was sick.

Owen pulled aside a curtain and looked down the hill. "There's nothing there."

She peered over his shoulder. The car was gone.

Russ lumbered across the room, the drink in his hand.

"Maybe you oughta be careful, you know? You think this is a safe neighborhood, but it's just what them guys go after, the money. You want to keep your doors locked, watch the kids."

"Watch yourself, too," Owen added. "I'd be in a mess without you."

"What do you think is going to happen to me?"

"You're alone here all day, aren't you?"

She looked about at the room, at the May sunshine pouring in through the windows. She could not imagine anyone coming into her home, not in the daytime, while she was there.

But there were the nights, too. Owen often stayed away till very late. She was alone with the children, and they were so young. The smile, which had begun when she thought of her sunny house, faded.

Owen looked grim. "Maybe we should get more insurance on the house. Probably for ourselves, too."

"Oh, that reminds me. Dad called. He has a favor to ask you."

"A big one?"

"Just medium-sized. He's going away for a couple of weeks to Florida. He wondered if you'd look in on his apartment. You know, feed the fish and water the plants. It doesn't have to be every day."

"Why go to Florida now?" Owen wondered. "Isn't this sort of off-season?"

"Well, why not? It's still nice there, and in winter he has all those subscriptions." She explained to Russ, "My dad's a theater buff. When Mom died he got an apartment right near Lincoln Center, and he always has at least half a dozen subscriptions."

He regarded her blankly. "Magazines?"

"No, plays, opera, ballet. Whatever they have at Lincoln Center."

A vague nod. Probably he had never heard of Lincoln Center. She turned back to Owen.

"I know it's out of your way, but could you? He doesn't know anybody else he can trust. All his friends are in Brooklyn."

To her gratification, Owen answered, "Sure, I'll do it."

"Thanks, hon."

"Don't call me 'hon.'"

He had an ulterior motive, as well as a certain regard for his father-in-law, in agreeing to look after the apartment. It was exceptionally convenient—in the heart of Manhattan, as the real estate ads liked to say—and he would have the place to himself in a large, impersonal building.

The day after Ruth's father left for Florida, Owen telephoned Lyn at her new office.

Her voice was cautious at first. "Who is this?" And then "*Owen?* Oh, my God!"

The "God" was on a watery note. He wondered if she was crying, or what this reaction meant.

"How are you doing?" He wanted to call her "darling," but the word did not come—yet.

"Okay." Still cautious. "What about you?"

"I'm all right. But I miss you."

"I miss you, too, Owen."

"Do you really?"

"I don't want to talk about it over the phone."

"That's exactly why I'm calling. Can I see you sometime? I have the use of a place here in town . . ."

It was not as easy as he had expected. He thought her husband would still be in school, but his classes had ended for the summer. She promised to make up a story about working late, and about the switchboard being turned off at five. She would make it foolproof, she said.

He would not take her out to dinner. That would only waste their time together. He bought a steak, a bottle of wine, and a container of Greek salad with dark olives and feta cheese. He waited for her outside the building so she would not have to explain herself to the doorman. He did not want word of this to get back to Tim, his father-in-law.

And then she came, and he felt something lighten in his heart as she walked toward him, a breeze blowing her long brown hair, her eyes full of eagerness.

"Owen, I *missed* you."

He took her elbow and hurried her inside, nodding to the doorman. She composed herself by the time they reached the elevator. As they rode to the eighth floor, with a soft background of canned music, she asked neutrally, "How are things at the office?"

"Not the same without you," he admitted. "And I mean that both personally and professionally."

"Did you get somebody else?"

"Yes, I got a girl from an agency, but it's not working out. I may have to let her go. How do you like your new job?"

The elevator stopped and opened. He steered her down the carpeted hallway toward his father-in-law's apartment.

"It's boring," she said. "It's another big place like the insurance company, and there aren't any people I really like."

She meant anybody like him. There were always Jackies and Dorises.

He unlocked the apartment. They entered a vestibule that opened out into the spacious living room with its greenery, its bubbling tank of tropical fish, and a view of Central Park.

"It's gorgeous!" she exclaimed. "Oh, this is really nice. I wish I could live in a place like this."

"You will, someday." He nibbled the top of her ear.

Very gently, she eased herself away.

"What's the matter?" he asked. "I thought you missed me."

"I do. But—I'm married." She turned and flung herself at him. "Owen, I'm so mixed up."

He led her to a large red couch. She did not even bother to look at the panorama of the park.

"What can I fix for you?" he asked, opening the cabinet where Tim kept his bar supplies.

"Vodka and tonic?"

He had forgotten to buy limes. She said it didn't matter. He poured their drinks and sat down with her on the sofa.

"Now, why are you mixed up?" he asked.

"About you and me."

"What's so confusing about us?"

"I guess it's mostly me. It doesn't bother you that you're married."

"If it bothers you, then why—"

"I told you. I wanted a family, not just an affair. And I can't have both. It doesn't work that way for me. I can't split myself in two pieces."

"People have been doing it since time began," he pointed out.

"Other people, but not me. I can't feel that way."

He helped her along. "It's all or nothing?"

She nodded.

"Then why did you agree to see me?"

She stared into her drink. Her mouth was turned down in a babyish way.

"Because I can't stop thinking about you."

"Look." He rested his arm on the back of the sofa, not quite touching her. "You married Jimmy just to get away from me, didn't you?"

"Joe," she corrected him.

"Okay, Joe. If you ask me, that's a damn silly reason to commit yourself like that. It's not fair to him and it's not fair to you. Because you're not really committed, are you?"

She looked up at him. He almost expected to see tears in her eyes, but there were none.

"I do love Joe," she said. "I mean—Well, it's different. I like my life with him, but it's not—It's not *you*."

"I'm not sure I know what you mean, exactly."

"All right, I'll spell it out. I wish I could be married to you instead of Joe."

There had not really been any need for her to say that, but it did something to him to hear the words.

"Well," he said.

"That's no answer."

"Answer?" It alarmed him. "What's to answer?"

"I don't know." She nestled against him. His arm slipped from the sofa back and encircled her.

"Lyn," he said, "let's take it one day at a time, okay? We don't know what might happen in the future. Even the near future. Let's just enjoy this—"

"But what about Joe?"

"You're the one who married Joe," he said. "Suppose you worry about him."

She tried to pull away. "That's not a very nice attitude."

"Sorry." He held her tightly and kissed her temple. "All I'm saying is, let's enjoy this evening. Let's forget our problems for a while. Everything might work out, who knows? Come on, let's have a good time."

He could feel her softening. He set down his drink and applied both arms to her. She did the same. To hell with the steak, he thought. There was always later. Or tomorrow. They were lucky to have this place. She could be on overtime for two whole weeks. If Joe Shmoe happened to get suspicious—

Well, even that, in the long run, might work to their advantage.

=9

For the next two weeks they met almost every evening at the apartment on Central Park West. She told Joe that her firm was busy with a very important project. For the government, she added. Secret war work.

She wondered if he could tell by looking at her that she had not been typing for the government. Her sister Beverly once said that it often showed on a woman's face when she had been, as Beverly put it, "with a man." If Joe had any suspicions, he never mentioned them.

Twice during the second week she typed so late that she was forced to spend the night at the apartment of a coworker (female) in Manhattan. She was careful to let him know each time, so he wouldn't worry.

"I really hate this," she told Owen after her call on the second occasion. "I hate lying."

"Tell him the truth, then." Owen lay naked on Tim Brandon's double bed. His body was more familiar to her than Joe's, and still handsome.

"What do you tell Ruth?" she asked.

"Nothing. She's the one who insisted on this caretaking bit. As for tonight, it's a lot more convenient to stay here in town than go all the way out to the island, don't you think? I might have done it for the whole two weeks."

"I guess it's easier for you, if you and Ruth are all washed up anyway," she said. "But I can't help feeling rotten about Joe. We just got married."

"Don't blame that on me, dear."

"I thought I was doing the right thing."

"You didn't think long enough. You shouldn't have tried to precipitate things."

He was absolutely right. She had acted too fast and made a mess of it. And now what? Was her whole life to be a mess?

She did not want to stay married to Joe, but she dreaded a divorce. She dreaded even discussing it with him. She would not be able to explain unless she told him the truth, and then he would be hurt and angry. With justification.

"If I leave him," she said slowly, "I'll be right back where I started. Except I wouldn't even be working for you."

He caught her hand. "Then come back and work for me. I told you I'm letting the new girl go."

"You said you might." She could not help smiling, although she fought against it. This was so irrelevant to the real problem.

"All right, I've made up my mind," he said. "I'll give her the word tomorrow. How about you?"

"Okay. I'll give *them* the word." She giggled as he pulled her down onto the bed.

That was their last full night together in the apartment. The next day she notified her employers that in two weeks she would be returning to her old job.

It was not so easy with Joe. She put off saying anything to him, because she did not know how to say it. In the process of stalling, and in her worry over how to make the break, she grew cooler and more distant.

"What's the matter with you?" he asked one night after they had made love. "You're a block of ice. Are you sick or something?"

"No, I'm okay." She struggled free of the tangled sheet and went to take a shower. The weather was hot and they were both bathed in sweat. Their bodies had slipped against each other like two wet eels. She had looked forward to her summer with Joe, the warm, easy nights, the pleasant times they would have, but now she felt impatient. It was mostly, she decided as she adjusted the shower, because she hadn't the courage to be honest with him.

She dried herself, put on her nightgown and went back to the bed, where he lay smoking. She reached across him to take a cigarette from his pack on the night table.

Silently he set the ashtray on the bed between them. Then he tugged at a strap on her nightgown.

"What are you wearing this for? It's a hot night."

"It feels better."

"Why? It'll make you sweat, and you just took a bath."

"Sometimes," she told him with a nervous edge to her voice, "I like to be covered."

He rolled over, resting on his elbow, and studied her.

"I want to ask you something. Now don't get mad."

"No, I'm not pregnant."

"That isn't what I wanted to ask."

He ground out his cigarette, and for a while, said nothing. She did not prompt him, for fear of what he would say. He continued to grind the cigarette long after it was out. Finally he dropped it and looked at her.

The only light in the room came from a street lamp shining through half-closed blinds. It made his eyes darkly brilliant, his face pale in the colorless gloom. There was a youthfulness about him that sometimes irritated her, but now it stabbed her. She did not want to hurt him, even as he spoke.

"Those nights you worked late and stayed in town," he said. "Was it really a girl from your office? Did you level with me?"

She felt choked with sickness and defeat. The moment she had dreaded was here.

She wanted to lie and put it off again and again.

She stared at the wall across from the bed. "No. I didn't level with you."

"Who was it, then?"

"Joe, I made a mistake. We shouldn't have gotten married."

"*Who was it?*"

She stared, seeing nothing but the wall, feeling his face close to hers. She wished it were not like this, with them in bed together, and he still naked.

"It was someone I care about very much," she answered. "I'm sorry, Joe. I tried. I wanted to be your wife—"

He loomed over her. She barely had time to be afraid before the blow came, making lights flash in her head. By the time she sat up, whimpering, holding her hand to her cheek, he was gone.

The legal part of her separation seemed to pass like something unreal and yet inevitable. It had all come about more quickly, more naturally, than she had expected, but emotionally it was harder than she had thought it would be. She had hurt Joe, and had not wanted to. She had hoped he would understand. She had even hoped that he might, himself, find someone else to love, and solve the problem for her.

She regretted, too, the loss of the good, innocent life they had led together. Once more she was cast into the sea, and again had no perceivable future.

But she could not give up Owen. He was what her life was all about.

Joe had long since moved out of the apartment, leaving her with a pleasant home which she could not afford on her single income, but she would never move back with her parents.

Owen urged her to keep the apartment. He told her he would help pay for it.

"I can't raise your salary to cover it," he explained. "Doris would know what you're getting. But I can slip it to you. Or even pay your landlord directly."

"It makes me feel cheap," she admitted. "But I don't know what else to do."

They were walking back to the office from lunch at Ricci's. He put his arm around her shoulder.

"Don't feel cheap. After all, as a businessman, I can't have a homeless secretary."

She smiled thinly. In spite of her misgivings, she was grateful. At least it made one less thing to worry about.

When Joe left, he had taken his car. She had no transportation but the public system, which was adequate, although the nearest subway stop was a fifteen-minute walk away. Still, she no longer had to walk late at night. Now that she had the apartment, there was no more need for drinks and dinner in public places, and furtive hotel rooms. Owen drove his car into the city several times a week, and they would go back together to her apartment.

"Maybe this is why I had to marry Joe," she remarked one evening as they relaxed in her living room in the breeze from an electric fan.

"*Had* to marry Joe?"

"So you and I could have this place to be together. It's like one of those things you just do, and then afterward there seems to be a reason for it."

She sat snuggled against him on the sofa. Her glass of ice water was two feet away, but she could not reach it without disturbing them both.

"I thought it was the other way around," he said. "I thought afterward there *didn't* seem to be any reason for it."

"Well . . ."

He lifted her away from him and leaned forward to add more ice to his drink.

"It's as silly as my own life."

"Your coexistence," she said. "Are you going to go on coexisting forever? Can't you just talk to her?"

"It's a little more complicated than that, dear. There are the children. And Ruth has money tied up in the business."

She did not pursue the subject. In a way, she could understand. The deeper the roots, the harder it was to dig them out.

But at least he wanted to dig. And someday he might begin.

Then there were other times, the times when he did not come. There was the Tuesday night that she waited for him to return to the office from an appointment. She forced herself to keep busy for the benefit of the others as they straggled out one by one: first Jackie, who dawdled over her filing, hoping to miss the subway rush, and in no particular hurry to get home because her policeman husband was on an evening shift; Mr. Tannen, delayed by a lengthy telephone call and forced to catch a later train; and finally the conscientious Doris.

"Aren't you leaving?" Doris asked as she slipped on her crocheted gloves. Doris always wore gloves, even in summer, to protect her hands from the germs of the subway.

"In a while," Lyn replied. "I have some things to finish first."

Doris eyed her curiously. This was uncharacteristic. Lyn nearly always left punctually, and then waited for Owen near the garage.

"They turn off the air conditioning at six-thirty, you know," Doris said. "Do you have keys for locking up?"

Lyn glanced at her watch. Six twenty-three. She felt a twinge of annoyance. He had said he would come.

"Yes, I have keys. Don't worry. Anyway, Mr. Holdridge isn't back yet. I guess I should wait for him."

Another curious look, but a rather more knowledgeable one this time. She knew they all suspected. Owen knew it, too. It was probably unavoidable, in that tiny office, but as long as no one actually mentioned it, he did not seem to mind.

"Where did he go?" Doris asked.

"He went to meet somebody. I think it's a buyer for the house on Spring Street."

"Are you sure you'll be all right?" Doris fished in her purse for the subway fare. "Keep the door locked. And it stays cool for a while after the air conditioning goes off, but then it gets stuffy."

She was gone. The office seemed a vacuum of silence. There was no way to reach Owen. As his secretary, she might have had an excuse for calling him, if she had known where he was.

He could not have forgotten. He was too sharp for that, and cared too much. He had never forgotten her yet.

She rarely noticed the constant blowing of the air conditioner, but she heard it when it went off. The other sounds in the building had died away, the voices as people left their offices, the opening and closing of the elevator doors, which made her look up each time, always to be disappointed. She hoped they kept the elevators running all night. Owen would have no way to get up without them. The fire stairs were locked on the outside at the ground floor.

Seven o'clock. She did not like the deserted office. Still, it was more comfortable than standing on the sidewalk and perhaps being mistaken for a hooker.

The telephone rang. She jumped, and with her heart beating wildly, picked it up.

"Lyn?" His voice was crisp and businesslike.

"Where are you?"

"I'm at a gas station. Honey, I'm sorry. Something came up. My kid broke his collarbone at day camp. I have to get home. I'm really sorry, okay? Thanks for waiting. I'll see you tomorrow."

She set down the phone. He *had* forgotten her. If he called from a gas station, it meant he was already on his way home. He might at least have let her know before he started.

She wondered how Ruth had reached him, and then realized he had probably called her to make his usual excuses.

Or maybe to check on them. Maybe he called just to check up now and then.

The air was hot and unbreathable as she covered her typewriter, turned out the lights, fastened the door's several locks, and started out to catch the subway home.

10

Now, through the window above her bed, she could see the brightness of true morning.

Painfully she turned her head and looked toward the door. She had not heard anything, but felt a prickling in her spine. An anticipation. A dread. She did not know what caused it. She watched the door to see whether it moved or anyone appeared. With her left hand she fumbled for the call button and held it ready.

But why? she wondered. *What am I afraid of?*

Yesterday someone had come in. And he had fled when she called for help.

Maybe only an orderly, looking for a purse to rob.

Yet her whole body told her differently. It was something she knew about, but could not remember.

She tried to think back from the present. A space of time seemed to be missing. She could remember Joe and the end of her marriage. She remembered Owen coming to her apartment during the summer.

But when was that summer? Was it long ago, or just last year? Or this year?

She remembered the lazy evenings, the occasional Saturdays. The times he had not been able to come, and her disappointment.

But he had made up for that. On a weekend in early fall they had gone away together and rented a bungalow at a resort. He had told his wife it was a real estate convention, and Ruth was too wrapped up in her home and children to be aware that it wasn't true.

How could she remember all that about Ruth and Owen and the children, and not know her own name? As though she did not belong, did not fit into the picture. As though she did not exist.

But she had been there. She remembered cooking for Owen, and he tossing the salad and helping to wash the dishes. It was almost as if they were married. But it was not as simple as when she and Joe decided to marry. There was Ruth, ever-present and blocking the way.

Ruth . . .

And yet, something must have happened. The nurse had called her Mrs. Holdridge. Did they change places?

Something happened to Ruth.

It pounded in her brain. Something happened, and Ruth was . . .

She remembered the first time she ever saw Ruth. The first and last. She had a picture in her mind of Ruth standing there in the office.

For a while the scene remained isolated. Then gradually it came back to her when it had happened.

It was in the fall, after that summer in her apartment. After the weekend at the resort.

He warned her that Ruth was coming that day.

"She's got a dentist appointment in the morning," he said, "and she's meeting me for lunch. Just thought I'd let you know."

"I'm glad you did." She felt suddenly breathless. "I'd probably faint if she walked in here and I didn't expect it."

Each time she heard the door open she would look up quickly, only to see a messenger, a delivery boy, or the postman. Finally it was none of those, but a small, rather plump woman in a navy blue suit, with short black hair and warm eyes.

The woman looked quickly around the office, taking in the two empty desks. Jackie and Doris were out to lunch. Her eyes grew wary as they lingered on Lyn. And Lyn knew who it was, and knew that Ruth knew who she was.

But this was not at all the way she had pictured Ruth—not this pleasant, hesitant woman with the heavy legs and cap of curly hair.

"Are you Mrs. Singleton?" the woman asked. It was a jolt to hear her say the name, which had been used so briefly.

"Yes, I am. May I help you?"

"I'm Ruth Holdridge. Is my husband in?"

"I think he's on the phone, Mrs. Holdridge. I'll go and tell him you're here. He's expecting you."

"Yes, of course he's expecting me. I'll go in myself." She glanced at the telephone on Lyn's desk, where a button glowed steadily, showing that one of the lines was in use. She took a breath and moved closer, fumbling uneasily with the catch on her purse.

Resolutely she began. "I've heard about you. Owen talks about you sometimes. I was wondering what you looked like."

Lyn wanted to speak, but could think of nothing to say.

"I know you got married," Ruth Holdridge continued, still tentatively, as though unsure of herself. "But then you separated."

"Yes—we did. It didn't work out."

"You didn't give it much time. Are you planning a divorce?"

"Yes, I think so." She knew so, but it seemed kinder not to say it.

She doesn't coexist, Lyn thought miserably. *A woman like that—She probably loves him.*

"And what are you going to do after that?" The voice was steadier now.

"I don't know. Go on working, I guess. At least I have a good job."

"I'm sorry you came back here."

Another jolt, emerging as it had from this deceptively timid and ladylike person.

Lyn answered as calmly as she could, "I'm a good secretary. He had problems with the other girl."

"I know. He told me you were a good secretary. That's what he kept trying to tell me, but the timing was very odd."

"What do you mean?"

"I'm sure you know what I mean." The voice went on, low and controlled, but there was tension in the face. Ruth's hands, clasping the navy blue purse, trembled with suppressed emotion.

"Everything about it," she went on. "The way you left here when you got married and came back as soon as you broke with your husband."

Again Lyn's mouth formed words that did not come. How much did the woman know? Did Owen talk about her all the time? He wouldn't, he couldn't. Or maybe—just enough to cover himself in case he mumbled her name in his sleep.

"Mrs. Holdridge, I had reasons of my own for changing jobs and for breaking up with my husband."

"I know you did. I know all about the reasons, and I think they concern me very much, and my children. I want you to know, Mrs. Singleton, I'm not going to let this happen to my children. They're his children, too. He's their father and they need him."

Lyn thought of the pent-up anger that must be there. Self-righteous anger. Her eyes wavered from the face, softly rounded and vulnerable, to the stocky body in that matronly suit. It reminded her, not of her mother, but of someone like her.

The door opened from the inner office.

"Ruth! I didn't know you were here. Why didn't somebody tell me?"

"You were on the phone," Lyn said dully.

Her tone deflated some of his false exuberance. He muttered, "Be right with you," and went back to put on his jacket. Dressed now, he took Ruth's arm in the tender manner he used so often with Lyn. Over his shoulder he threw Lyn a look that was blank and yet somehow filled with meaning, and then they were gone.

He loved her, that was what he meant, no matter what Ruth might say or do to her. He must have realized there had been some kind of confrontation, and it surprised him. In the blind way of men, he had assumed that Ruth was ignorant of the affair, probably because she never mentioned it. He had underestimated his wife, even her ability to figure out a threat to her marriage and children.

Lyn felt depressed, in spite of the message of love he had sent her. It had been different when Ruth was only a picture in her mind—and, as it turned out, an inaccurate one. She had imagined a haughty, tweedy blond; a cold, wealthy suburbanite who had everything she wanted, and therefore deserved to be resented.

One who would have demolished her and not been afraid of her. Or perhaps what Ruth feared was her own anger. She was too gentle for this. Too nice a person for all that was happening to her.

Damn. She had made a mistake in her typing. Left out a phrase. It would have to be done over.

She had not yet had lunch, but was no longer hungry. Especially when she would have to eat alone.

Did Ruth, she wondered, often feel alone?

Ruth went to Altman's after lunch, but her heart was not in shopping. She looked for something to buy for herself. She deserved a treat. Something to make her feel pretty.

She had never been thrilled with her looks, but it hadn't mattered before. Now she needed to be more than adequate. She needed a doll-like face and soft hair waving about her shoulders.

And long, slender legs. You could see, even under the desk,

that Lyn Singleton had long, slender legs. She was that kind of build.

After wandering back and forth past counters of accessories and cosmetics, and not really noticing anything because she was too dissatisfied with herself to know what she wanted, Ruth bought a tie for Owen and a tan suede purse for Tina.

For Dennie, she picked out a baseball glove. He already had one, but they had gotten a large size so he could grow into it, and he found it too loose.

She tried on dresses, hostess gowns, even a coat. Nothing looked right on her. *She* was not right. Beside her, in every mirror, stood a long-legged girl . . .

And yet she had not been a slick sort of girl, the kind you would imagine as a homewrecker. Probably she really thought she loved him, but it wasn't fair. It wasn't fair to be thirty-seven and have this girl who was only twenty . . . It just wasn't fair.

After an equally uninspired visit to Lord and Taylor, she walked along Thirty-fourth Street to Penn Station, where she waited for Owen at his usual train gate.

Usual? At least it had been until a few months ago. She wondered where that girl lived, that he found it expedient now to drive his car into town most days and pay for garaging it.

She wondered what kind of girl would carry on an affair with someone else's husband. Why wasn't she capable of finding a man of her own, or of holding the one she had? It was some kind of psychological problem, Ruth imagined. A father fixation, perhaps.

She ought to have gotten tougher with her. But the idea of screaming, "Keep your hands off my husband!" was ludicrous. She could not picture herself talking like that, even if it was what she really meant.

Then she saw Owen coming through the crowd and smiling when he caught sight of her. She smiled back. He twined his arm around hers and took her hand as they walked through the gate to the train.

"Did you have a good afternoon?" he asked.

"Oh, so-so. I bought a few things for you and the kids."

He was the one who had suggested that they go home together. Perhaps he would rather have seen the girl. This might have been his idea of an obligation.

But he acted as though he enjoyed it. The whole day. So maybe he cared about her after all. Maybe the girl was just something he had to do, a last grasp at youth. Some men were like that. They couldn't let go.

His hand released hers so they could board the train. She gave his an affectionate pat as she moved ahead of him. It was funny how transparent men were. Such children.

Lyn rode the subway alone, thinking of Owen and Ruth together on the train. Going home. Their home was a real one, not just a place to live.

She could not stop thinking of Ruth. It was always a shock when people turned out differently from what one expected. And it was a further shock to have seen in Ruth, not the rival she had pictured, but someone she could almost equate with her mother. Perhaps because of that suit and the heavy hips.

So he hadn't been frozen out by a chilly aristocrat. He had never put it that way, it was only what she imagined, especially after seeing Ruth's father's apartment.

Perhaps he had only been bored.

But that couldn't be it. He was really in love. And he didn't love Ruth—at least not in the same way.

And Ruth? What about her? She had sworn she was going to fight for Owen, but not because she loved him. Only because of the children. Yet Owen had needs, too. The children would get over their parents' divorce. Children always did, as far as she knew. Anyway, they had the whole rest of their lives. Owen's time was shorter, and he deserved some happiness.

The next evening, as they were riding out to Elmhurst on the Long Island Expressway with the sun setting behind them in a smoggy red blaze, he startled her by asking what she had thought of Ruth.

"I thought she was kind of cute," Lyn replied, "until she started lecturing me. And—I don't know how to describe it. Sort of middle-aged. More than you."

"More than me?"

"You're not middle-aged at all."

"She's only thirty-seven."

"That's what I mean. She looked older. I was surprised."

"What's this about her lecturing you?"

"Well, she did. About you. Not yelling or screaming, or any-thing, but she meant it."

"I didn't think she knew who you were."

"She knows more than you think. You must have talked about me quite a lot. She knows exactly when I got married and when I got separated, and when I quit and came back."

"Of course. You're my secretary. That's the only context I ever mentioned you in. She always wants to know what's hap-pening at the office."

"I almost wish I hadn't seen her."

"Why?"

He had been intent upon the conversation and nearly missed the Elmhurst exit. He turned suddenly at the last moment. Lyn gripped the edge of the seat, then replied, "She didn't look like what I expected, and she didn't look happy. I don't want to make her miserable. I really don't."

He grinned. "You just wish she'd see it our way."

"Well, yes. I really mean it. If my husband was in love with another woman, I'd get him out so fast . . ."

"Some women don't want to give up the status they have from being married, even if it's all they have."

"You'd think they'd have a little pride. Anyway, marriage should be more than that. If I were her, I'd divorce you and find somebody I could have a real marriage with."

He laughed softly. She wondered if perhaps it was too late for Ruth to find anybody, and that, again, made her feel guilty.

Probably, in Ruth's eyes, Lyn was the one who ought to find somebody else and have a real marriage.

When they reached her building, she looked around, as always, to see if anyone was watching. Not that it mattered. She only felt that they must guess at her relationship with him, and it embarrassed her. She wished it could be open and legal.

An hour later, as the lambchops broiled, she sat beside him on the sofa, drinking Seven-Up while he had whiskey and soda. The specter of Ruth would not go away.

"She's a nice woman," Lyn said. "There's got to be some way—some *nice* way—Well, I wish she'd just understand."

"That would make it simpler, wouldn't it?" He tilted his half-empty glass, watching the ice cubes slide in one direction and then another.

"Don't make fun of me. I just meant—I know it's hard for her. I guess, either way, a woman's got to lose her pride, whether she gives up or hangs on. But she didn't sound as if it's because she wants you. It's for the children."

"I must say, that bothers me, too," he said. "I'd hate to lose them. But there's another thing, at least from my point of view. I told you about that. A number of the properties are in her name. Of course, once those are sold . . ."

"Why did you do it that way?"

"Several reasons, some having to do with taxes and some with the fact that she's one of the backers of the business."

The backer, Lyn thought bitterly. She knew by now that most of the money to launch the business had come from Ruth. She ought to have been glad, knowing that Ruth's value was more in her money than in herself, but it seemed as though Ruth had the situation pretty well sewed up.

"That means no divorce, right?"

"Darling, don't talk like that. You're putting words in my mouth. It's just that, right now—"

"Right now," she knew, could last a very long time. Maybe forever. She could not go on like this all her life, but the prospect of finding someone else to love was unthinkable.

11

Another liquid meal. It consisted of broth, tea, and a glass of chocolate-flavored sludge. At least it was chocolate color. The aide who came to help her said it was fortified milk.

It tasted more than fortified. It was bitter, as though they had forgotten to sweeten the chocolate. But it was scarcely a gourmet treat anyway, and her mouth still tasted metallic from the injuries. She drank a third of it and turned her head away refusing the rest.

The aide had left and her tray had been removed, when she began to feel sick.

No, she thought, fighting the nausea. *I can't.*

She was already miserable enough. *Please, God, you can't do this to me!* She could not throw up, not with broken ribs and a wired jaw.

But the sickness rushed forward, gripping her. She rolled her head on the pillow and moaned aloud, too distraught to think of anything but that it must stop. Only when her body began to heave did she remember the call button.

She groped for it. It was not there. She cried out again. Her cry was broken as bitter fluid spilled from her mouth.

Again and again the nausea racked her. There was no more liquid to lose, but her body fought on apart from her conscious mind, which grew hazy with pain and exertion. Through the haze she saw a face with widened eyes. A dark face, reflecting her own agony. And then she slipped away.

When she woke, Owen sat beside her bed, holding her hand. "Thank God," he said as she opened her eyes.

He stroked her hair. "They called me. I was about to leave the house, and they said you'd gone into convulsions. My God, baby, I thought—You're all right now, aren't you?"

He continued to stroke her forehead. His words sounded strange to her, meaningless and artificial. They did not sound the way Owen talked. Perhaps it was only a part of her general condition. Nothing tasted right, either.

"This has been hell," he said. "The kids miss you. I miss you. They said you might be here a couple of weeks."

She would be here forever. She felt as though she would never be able to walk again, or get up off the bed.

And this morning—she thought it was still the same day—this morning, the sudden nausea, the violent vomiting, and he had said she had had convulsions.

It was poison. The drink was poisoned.

She wanted to tell him. About the man behind the door, and then this morning.

But she could do nothing. Although the man had failed twice, in the end he would get her, because she was helpless.

Why? Why does he want to hurt me?

She could not remember ever knowing such a man, but those winged eyebrows—She remembered—

Nothing. She only *knew*.

Owen sat holding her hand, patting and stroking it. It was her left hand, stiff, but free of bandages. Could she use it to write a note? Tell him in clumsy, left-handed scrawl about the man who tried to kill her?

She needed something to write on. She tried to pull her hand away from his, to tell him with gestures that she needed to write. He held on tightly.

"Poor baby," he said, patting her again.

She tried to say his name, to speak to him. If she forced herself . . .

She could only make an inarticulate sound.

He looked at her with concern. "Poor baby. I'm so sorry. I'll go and find somebody."

He left the room, and returned a few minutes later.

"I asked them to give you something for the pain. They'll be here right away."

She tried again. *No, no, no!* Her mouth would not form the words.

No, I mustn't sleep. Don't make me sleep.

She fought against the nurse who came with a needle. Tears welled in her eyes.

"God, it must be awful," Owen said through the blur. He took her hand again and held it while she sobbed.

Was it like this for Ruth—that other time? The terror, the dread. Knowing what was to come and not being able to stop it.

How much did she know? Or did they take her by surprise?

She remembered that autumn. They went away again for another weekend. He told Ruth he was looking at some places in the country. And he was, although with no intention of investing. He was looking at a small hotel in the Catskills, with fiery autumn colors, and evergreens, and Lyn.

There was not much to do in the fall. The swimming pool had been emptied and the summer festivities were over, but they took walks in the woods, where they could be together in mountain air. She could sleep in the same bed with him all night, and that was precious.

They were walking on a mountain trail in the balmy afternoon. He held her hand as they stumbled through a rocky gully, a dry brook bed.

"I love this," she told him. "I love this weekend, but I want it to be real. If we could be together like this all the time, without feeling guilty—It's like I'm borrowing you, and the worst part is knowing it will all end tomorrow."

"It's not going to end," he said, laughing as he lifted her up over a steep and slippery boulder.

"Yes, it will. I'll have to go back to my apartment. It's not so bad for you. You have a family."

He stopped her and held her. She could feel his eagerness. He wanted her right there, under the red leaves.

"You'll have a family. We'll have each other very soon. Just trust me. "

She trusted him. It couldn't take even a year to sell the few buildings that were in Ruth's name. And if he got Ruth to agree, and they had a quickie divorce instead of a long, drawn-out hassle, then in just a few months maybe he and she could be married.

She imagined an apartment in Manhattan, something like the one where Ruth's father lived. On one or two weekends a month his children would come to visit, and they would go to the zoo and have lunch on the terrace there, and visit the top of the Empire State Building, and take the Circle Line boat around the island of Manhattan. All the things she had never done. It would be more fun with the children.

They came to an overlook at the side of the mountain. The valley was spread before them, an incredible checkerboard of red and yellow, green and brown.

"It's just like a painting!" she exclaimed. "You know, as if they splotched on the color. You never see any autumn colors in the city. I'm so glad we came."

"I'm glad, too, baby." He studied the scene through binoculars, and she studied him. He wore tan corduroy pants and a heavy Aran sweater, and he looked more attractive than ever.

"Can we come here again sometime?" she asked.

"Of course. We'll do all these things, as soon as we can be together legally."

The next day, during the trip home, he said it again. "When we can be together legally."

It's going to happen, she thought. *He really means it.*

He was paving the way financially, selling the buildings owned by Ruth. The only unpredictable factor was Ruth herself, and he seemed confident that even that could be solved.

It was solved in a way that neither of them could have foreseen. She found it unbelievable, even as events moved on from there, confirming what had happened. She had never lived a nightmare before.

The morning was an unusual one to begin with. He had needed some documents picked up from an office in Queens, and had sent her home early the previous afternoon so that she could collect them on her way and bring them to the office in the morning.

"I'd go myself," he had said, glancing at his watch, "but I have an appointment with a buyer. I hate to do this to you. It means an extra subway ride. Oh, hell, take a taxi." And he had given her a ten-dollar bill.

She had not used the money, because she couldn't find a taxi.

The next morning he telephoned her at seven o'clock, just as she was waking.

"Did you get the papers? Good. I have to sign them, have one of them notarized, and drop them off, so I might as well stop by your place, then look for a notary. Is eight okay?"

"But Mr. Tannen's a notary." How could he have forgotten?

"I'm not sure, but I think his license may have expired. Anyway, since they have to be delivered, we can do it all in one trip. You'll have a ride to work the long way around."

She liked that idea. A ride to work was better any time than the subway, and she never got over her pleasure in his large, luxurious car with its comfortable seats and elaborate dashboard.

When he arrived, she was ready to leave, but he insisted upon examining the papers to be sure every detail was satisfactory.

"How about some coffee, then?" she asked. "I'm sorry, I'm all out of regular."

"Instant's fine." He looked up belatedly as she started toward the kitchen. They smiled at each other, and he went back to his reading.

She knew what would happen. They would make love. And

they would walk into the office together at ten o'clock, and the others would think he had spent the night with her.

She was right. He drank his coffee while he finished perusing the papers, and then they made love.

He was dressing in the bathroom when he called out to her, "Oh, hey, would you do something for me? Would you get Ruth on the phone?"

"Right now? From here?"

"She won't know where we are. I don't want to put it off. She wasn't feeling well this morning. I'd like to find out how she is."

She remembered his number, although she rarely had occasion to dial it. Ruth answered almost immediately.

"Mrs. Holdridge?" Lyn kept her voice businesslike. "Your husband would like to talk to you. Just a moment, please."

The conversation was brief. She tried not to listen, but heard him asking, "Is everything okay? Just checking. . . . Well, why not? Because I love you, okay?"

She hurried into the kitchen, for no reason except to be discreet, and because it hurt her to hear him say he loved someone else. Even his wife. Of course he didn't mean it.

Without warning, he came up behind her and put his arms around her. "Ready to go?"

"Just a second." A last-minute check to be sure the windows were closed, the stove turned off. Not until they were in the car did she ask about the call. "How was Ruth? Is she feeling better?"

"I guess so. She sounded better. It's probably just a sinus infection."

He found a notary public at a small tax office in Long Island City. It was after ten o'clock by the time they crossed the Queensboro Bridge. He told her it was a good thing they had stopped to make love; by now the traffic was much lighter.

He headed downtown on Second Avenue, and there they encountered very slow traffic. He cursed himself aloud and wished he had taken the FDR Drive instead. Past Forty-

second Street, the traffic thinned. Lyn sat back, smoked a cigarette, and enjoyed the ride. It was a harmless way to be late for
work. She only dreaded the moment when they would walk in
together.

"Maybe you should have dropped me off," she said. "It's
going to look awfully funny, both of us coming in an hour
late."

He shook his head. "I need you to sit in the car while I run
up with these things. No way I can park there legally."

She saw what he meant when they finally stopped in front of
a low office building on Nineteenth Street, in a block clogged
with trucks trying to back into loading docks, and No Parking
signs everywhere. She waited in the car with instructions to
drive around the block if necessary. She disliked the thought
of driving such a beautiful car, perhaps scratching it on a
skew-wise truck, but he returned before it became necessary.

He drove back uptown, parked in his usual garage, and they
stopped for coffee at a luncheonette.

When they were on their way to the office, she tried again.
"Maybe I'd better go ahead—"

He tucked her hand under his arm, as though to hold her in
place.

"Don't you worry about it. Our program this morning was
perfectly logical and aboveboard, except for one little lapse
that nobody knows about. If you start carrying on as if we did
something wrong, people will think we did something wrong,
so just relax."

She was not sure it was that simple, but let it go. Being married, he had more at stake than she. It was only what Jackie
and Doris would think that bothered her.

When they entered the office, Jackie was not at her desk—
probably in the restroom—and Doris barely glanced at them.
Lyn was not fooled by Doris's apparent lack of notice. Doris
noticed everything, but her discretion smoothed over the awkward moment, and Lyn sat down gratefully at her own desk.

Half an hour later, when Owen called her in to discuss the

day's mail, she thought he seemed preoccupied. It occurred to her that it might be an act to demonstrate a lack of interest in her for Mr. Tannen's benefit.

"I have a luncheon appointment today," Owen said, turning a page of his desk calendar, "at one-thirty. And tomorrow Ruth is coming in to sign over one of the buildings, so I'll be having lunch with her. I wanted to go and check on those two houses in the Bronx, but that might have to wait till next week." He scribbled something on the calendar, and out of Mr. Tannen's sight, patted her knee. Even that seemed mechanical.

When she left his office with the day's dictation, she saw him look at his watch. She sat down at her own desk and began the first letter. Jackie asked her where she had been that morning.

"All over," she replied. "The boss gave me some papers to deliver. I had to go downtown." The answer satisfied Jackie, and apparently Doris.

It was nearly one o'clock, and only she and Owen remained in the office, when the telephone rang. She picked it up. "T and H Realty."

Someone was breathing hard, almost gasping. "Owen—Is Mr. Holdridge there?"

"May I ask who's calling, please?"

It was a woman. Her voice trembled. "Just get Mr. Holdridge. This is an emergency."

Alarmed, she put the call on hold and notified Owen. "They say it's an emergency."

Through the open door she heard him answer, heard him say over and over again, "My God. Oh, my God. Are you sure? Oh, my God."

He spoke for a few moments longer, then came out of his office, slipping on his suit jacket.

"I've got to go home, Lyn. Something's happened to Ruth."

He was gone before she could ask any questions. She collected herself and cancelled his luncheon appointment. Then she sat at her desk, watery and frightened, not knowing what

to do. It had sounded terrible, whatever it was. A terrible accident. Perhaps a car wreck. Maybe she was already dead.

She was alone in the office, waiting to hear more, and knowing it would be a long time. She wished she could have gone
with him. He would need someone, but of course that would
be impossible.

Promptly at one-thirty, as she always did, Doris returned
from lunch. She was unpinning the little old-fashioned hat
from the back of her head when Lyn said, "Mr. Holdridge had
to go home. Something happened to his wife."

Doris turned, her round eyes bulging. "What? Do you know
what it was? Is it serious?"

"That's all I know. He rushed out. Someone called him, a
woman. She sounded upset."

"Oh, dear, I hope it's not serious." Doris sat down weakly.

Jackie came in from lunch, and finally Mr. Tannen. By then,
Doris was taking it upon herself to make the announcement,
leaving Lyn to fill in nonexistent details. Mr. Tannen dialed
the Holdridge home and spoke briefly to someone. He looked
up at the three women, all the twinkle gone from his elfin face.

"That was a policeman," he said in disbelief. "She's dead. A
burglary."

"Dead?" screamed Doris.

Lyn felt her face go white, her muscles again turn to water.
"Poor Owen," she murmured, inadvertently using his first
name.

Jackie barely glanced at her. "Do you mean somebody actually broke in and *killed* her?" she demanded of Mr. Tannen.
"When, last night?"

"This morning. The kid discovered it when she came home
for lunch."

"Oh, no." Lyn slipped back to her desk, her stomach churn-
ing. She thought of the child in that picture, finding her
mother dead. Shot or stabbed, perhaps, with splashes of blood.
He did say "she." So it was not the little boy, the one she had
seen running down the hill.

"I just don't believe it," she said aloud, and looked up to find Jackie standing by her desk, watching her curiously.

"Did you know her?" Jackie asked.

"I met her once when she came in here. She was—kind of cute."

A strange day . . . a strange day . . . driving around with Owen while his wife was being murdered. And making love to him.

I wonder if I'll go to hell, she thought.

It occurred to her that probably Owen was in hell right now. She wondered when she would see him again. Who would look after his children?

Dimly she became aware that Mr. Tannen had spoken to her. He asked, "You okay, Lyn?"

She stared at him and did not answer, not knowing what to say. All three of them were watching her.

She managed to reply, "Well, I guess I'm just shocked."

"I think we all are," he said. "I'd close the office, but there'll be people calling and coming in. They'd expect somebody to be here."

In other words, she must pull herself together. He could not know how shocked she was, how confused, thinking back to that unusual morning.

The telephone rang. She answered it. An insurance company, asking about a tardy payment on a building that had long since changed hands. The business day had resumed with scarcely a stammer.

12

Ruth was buried on Sunday. The next day, Owen returned to the office. Even with his face lined and pale, he looked handsome.

Within a few minutes of his arrival, he called Lyn to come in and discuss the day's work. It was the first time they had been together since the morning of the tragedy.

"I want to tell you this while I have a chance," he said, meaning before Mr. Tannen came in. "They're investigating what happened, of course, and they may be asking you some questions."

She was stunned. "Me? Why me?"

He put his hand over hers. "Not anything to do with you, darling. I didn't mean to frighten you. It just seems that every time there's a homicide, one of the first people they question is the spouse. I tried to keep you out of it. I don't think they know much about us, but they still might want to talk to you."

She moistened her lips. "What shall I say?"

"It's probably best to tell them the truth. It doesn't matter what the police know about us, as long as the press doesn't get hold of it."

"But they will. The press gets hold of everything."

There had been newspaper stories about the murder, but she had not given much thought to the fact that she herself might be part of it.

He asked, "Did you tell anyone I was with you that morning?"

"No . . ." She tried to think. Had she? Had anyone asked?

"Then don't. That's the time they'll concentrate on, and they'll probably assume I spent the night with you."

"I know."

"Don't tell them anything, in fact. Let them dig. There's no reason why you should hand over your reputation. We'll try to keep you out of it as much as we possibly can."

She nodded obediently, imagining her parents reading about her in the newspaper (". . . his secretary, who was also his mistress . . .").

Then she clutched at his hand, whimpering. "It's so terrible for you."

Grimly, he agreed. "Just when it was all working out. She was almost halfway going along with the idea of a divorce. Now we have this mess. We'll have to stop seeing each other for a while. But the worst part is the kids."

"How are they taking it?"

"How do you think? They're destroyed. And Tina, my God. Of all the things to happen. Usually we have a housekeeper come in a couple of mornings a week. She couldn't make it that day, kept phoning and phoning, trying to get Ruth. And then Tina, poor kid, had a half day at school. Looked forward to her afternoon off. Oh, God." He dropped his face into his hand.

She wanted to hold him and comfort him, but that was out of the question now. She would not be able to hold him for a long time.

"If the housekeeper had been there," she said, "maybe—"

He shook his head. "You never know. The housekeeper doesn't come until ten. They think it happened before that. Or if she'd been there, he might have gotten them both."

"Before ten? But you called her just at nine!"

"I suppose it doesn't take long." He stared at the desk, his face set. "He could have been lurking even then. Heard her talking on the phone."

She knew from the news reports that Ruth had been bludg-
eoned. How long did it take to batter a woman to death?

"Anyhow," he said, "before we start on the mail, I'd like you
to do something for me. I have an associate downtown who's
been waiting for some papers. His actual office is in Brooklyn,
but I'm not going to ask you to make that long a trip, so he's
agreed to meet you at one of his habitual hangouts. It's a place
called Moylan's, and it's perfectly respectable, even though
you'll probably be the only woman there, but you don't have to
stay any longer than it takes to deliver this package." He
unlocked the center drawer of his desk and took out a manila
envelope, fat with the documents inside it and tightly sealed
with brown tape.

"What is it?" she asked.

He caught his breath, perhaps in impatience. "I told you, it's
some papers. I didn't get to it sooner, for obvious reasons, but
they have to reach him today."

"No, I mean this Moylan's place, if I'm the only woman
there."

"Oh, it's a bar. Nothing terrible. A perfectly respectable bar.
It's only that I thought you might feel a little odd going in
there in the morning."

"That's all right." She would do anything to help him.

"Good girl. I appreciate this." He scribbled an address on
the envelope and described the man she was to look for.

Moylan's was on Greenwich Avenue in the lower part of the
Village. She found its door standing open on that mild November morning, letting out sweet alcoholic fumes. As her eyes
adjusted from the outside light, she studied the shapes
hunched over the bar, or clustered in conversation at one end
of it. What had appeared to be a roomful of men was only
about half a dozen.

One was a hulk with black curly hair, a brown suit and pink
sports shirt. He was sitting on a stool so she could not see his
height, but he looked big, and he watched her with interest.

"Mr. Jaeger?" she asked.

"Yeah. Whadda you want?"

"I have something for you from Mr. Holdridge." She held out the envelope.

He beckoned her closer. "Oh ho, my buddy finally got smart. I thought he was holdin' out on me."

He took the envelope from her. As she turned to leave, he called after her, "Hey, sugar, what's your name?"

"I'm Mr. Holdridge's secretary," she answered.

"Yeah, I know, but I asked your name."

She wondered if he was anyone important to Owen's business. He did not seem like the type at all, but you never could tell. She dared not be rude to him.

"I'm Mrs. Singleton. It was nice meeting you." She backed toward the door.

"Come and have a drink with me, Mrs. Singleton. This is a big occasion."

All the men were watching her, some of them smirking. Again she tried to conceal her revulsion.

"Thanks, but I have to get back to work. Maybe another time."

She had been moving as she spoke, and now was outside. She hurried toward the subway. The entire episode made her ill, and she could not understand quite why. She had met offensive people before. She had been invited for drinks before, and even propositioned. Perhaps it was because of his connection with Owen. She felt that she wanted to protect Owen, even more than herself, from being sullied.

When she entered the office, Owen looked up questioningly. He did appear pale, she noticed for the second time that morning, and even a little older. He had been under a terrible strain.

"Are you sure you delivered it to the right person?" he asked.

Startled, she replied, "He was the one who looked like what you said, and he answered to the name. He seemed to be expecting it, too."

"What do you mean?"

"He said, 'My buddy finally got smart.' And then he said, 'I thought he was holding out on me.'"

"He said that, huh?"

"And he asked me to stay for a drink."

"He's a snake. You didn't take him up on it, I hope."

She agreed emphatically that she had not, and tried to describe her impression of Mr. Jaeger. Owen, apparently satisfied that all had gone well, picked up the telephone and began dialing.

She was hurt. He had never done that before, cut her off when she was speaking, even if it wasn't important.

Probably, she decided as she went back to her desk, it was his dazed state of mind. Probably, also, he was trying to keep a distance between them.

The questions began that evening. A detective called her at home and said he would like to come and speak with her.

"We just want to check a few things," he added, as though to reassure her.

She had not needed reassuring until he said that. Check what? It occurred to her that if they knew she was Owen's girlfriend, they might think she had something to do with the killing.

It was seven o'clock. She had lingered at the office, ready with the consolation and support she knew he must need. Finally he had spoken almost harshly to her. "Will you go on home? I told you, we have to play this thing down."

And so she had left, still wanting desperately to be with him. She could tell he was worried. It had been in his voice. She wondered why he himself did not want to hurry home to his children.

Again, as she waited for the police investigators, she heard the words and felt her own hurt at the sound of them. But he was the one who was really hurt. He had just lost his wife, the mother of his children, and now, instead of letting him work through his grief and patch up the family disruption, they hounded him with questions.

She had not had time to eat, and didn't feel like it. She felt, by the time the doorbell rang, as though her throat was stuffed with cotton.

Outside her door stood two men in business suits. "Mrs. Singleton?" one of them asked. "I'm Lieutenant Farley. We'd like to talk to you for a minute."

She stood aside to admit them. Probably here, in her own home, she could manage. It would be different if they took her to a police station.

They were both big men with similar, cleancut faces. It was all she noticed of them as they entered her living room, seeming to fill and dominate the space where she had spent so much time with Owen.

"You work in the office of T and H Realty as a secretary," Farley began. "Are you secretary to Mr. Holdridge?"

She cleared her throat. "To both. Mr. Holdridge and Mr. Tannen. But mostly I work with Mr. Holdridge."

She wondered if Doris and Jackie were being questioned, too, and what they would say. They must certainly have guessed about Owen and herself, but they didn't know for sure. How much would they tell?

"Do you often work late?"

"Sometimes." Her mouth felt dry. She did not care about herself, only about Owen.

"Were you working late on the night of November fifth?"

"No, I—In fact, I left early. I had to pick up some papers. They were—on my way."

"Where was that?"

"Woodside."

"Who asked you to do this?"

"Mr. Holdridge."

"Does he often send you on errands like that?"

"Sure. On errands, yes. That was the first time in the evening, but you see, it was on my way home."

"Did you see Mr. Holdridge at any time during the evening of November fifth? No? What time did you see him the next morning?"

She opened her mouth. Was this a trap?

"After—when I got to the office. It must have been eleven-thirty or twelve. I had to deliver the papers first to a place downtown."

"You arrived at the office between eleven-thirty and twelve. Could you be more specific about that?"

"No, I couldn't."

"Was Mr. Holdridge there when you arrived?"

Again her mouth opened wordlessly. They could ask Jackie or Doris what time he came in, and perhaps already had.

"Actually, we ran into each other on the way up. We went in together."

"Did anyone see you go in together?"

"Yes. Doris Peltzer."

"You saw quite a lot of Mr. Holdridge, didn't you, since you started working for him?"

"Every day. Except for a while when I went to work in another place. An engineering firm."

"Why did you go to work in another place and then return to T and H Realty?"

"Because—I got married. I thought it was better."

"Why did you think it was better?"

They knew. They knew.

"Well, you see, I was getting a little too involved with Mr. Holdridge, and he was a married man. I thought it was better to make a clean break."

"Is that why you married someone else?"

"Well, partially. And I wanted a life of my own. I mean—a family."

She wondered if they had the right to ask her such questions. Of course they wanted to establish that he had a girl-friend. Or—she hated the word—a mistress. It would make a strong case against him.

"Are you still married to Joseph Singleton?" Farley inquired.

"No, we broke up."

"Are you divorced? When and where did you get your divorce?"

"Joe did. He went to Mexico. You can ask him for the details, if you need them."

They obtained Joseph Singleton's address and then they left, after advising her that there might be further questions.

She locked the door and returned to the pool of light in her living room. She sat down in a black canvas chair, curling her legs under her.

They had asked hardly anything. It was as though they knew it already. All of it.

They couldn't really suspect him. For one thing, they must have known what time he left home that morning. The children could have told them that.

She wondered if possibly they might suspect her. But they hadn't asked for corroboration of her statement that she had delivered the papers downtown. If they did, they would find out it was Owen who had delivered them, and then he would be cleared, and that was the most important thing. In fact, there was no real danger for either of them, since they were innocent.

An anonymous, faceless burglar. Maybe they would never find him. It was probably easier to try to pin it on Owen. But they couldn't.

After two more weeks of investigation, she found that they could. Owen Holdridge was arrested and charged with the murder of his wife.

13

The trial was set for June. During the legal maneuvering that preceded it, Owen continued his daily routine as though nothing had happened. Henry Tannen suggested a leave of absence so that he could prepare his case.

"Can't afford to take the time off," was Owen's reply. He saw no need to prepare a case when the prosecution had none.

Yet the story he told was damning, Lyn felt, as long as he continued to leave her out of it. What other alibi did he have for the crucial time span? To account for his coming late to the office, he told the investigators that he had driven off the Long Island Expressway to change a tire. The police set up roadblocks and questioned daily travelers, but on the morning of November sixth, no one had seen a man changing a tire.

She begged to be allowed to tell the truth. He was adamant. He would not, he said in one of their rare moments together, allow anyone to drag her through the mud.

"It won't work," she insisted. "It's just not that easy. Look how thorough they are—roadblocks and everything. They'll ask the people at the place where you delivered those papers."

"I doubt if it'll even get that far," he chuckled, and patted her arm reassuringly.

She needed reassurance. She was alone, facing a storm that involved her as much as it did him. The only place where she could see him was the office. He told her that if they met outside, they would certainly be observed. Furthermore, he said, their telephones were probably bugged. The prosecution would try to pile up everything it could, including their relationship and whatever they might say to each other.

The worst part of it came, as she had feared it might, when the trial opened. She was subpoenaed to appear as a witness for the prosecution. She would be on display, bared to the public as the Other Woman.

The term had not been used—at least not yet, but she braced herself. She knew how people's minds worked.

She had never felt like the Other Woman. She was only herself, and it was not her fault that she had fallen in love with him and he with her. The only pity of it was Ruth, who had not deserved a brutal death on top of the breakup of her marriage. A terrible, terrible pity. But that, too, was fate. No one could have known it would happen, and therefore no one could have prevented it.

She would have to dress carefully for the trial. Her image was important. She tried on a slim green dress with a V-neckline and a pearl choker. It was too sexy.

A high-collared blouse with a bow at the throat. Too demure. Nothing could be worse than to look like a mistress who was trying not to look like a mistress.

A secretary. That was what she was. An efficient businesswoman. She decided on a beige linen-look suit with a smooth cream-color blouse.

They were coming to pick her up in a car. She did not know whether that was the usual procedure, but was glad she did not have to take the train.

She tried to eat breakfast. All she could manage was half a cup of instant coffee. She was ready when a young woman from the District Attorney's office rang her doorbell.

"I hope you realize," she told the young woman as she got into the car, "that I'm not on your side, even if I'm supposed to testify for you. I know Mr. Holdridge better than you do, and I think you're trying to railroad him. You just have to pin it on somebody."

The woman smiled. She was unpolished and friendly-looking, and wore heavy-rimmed glasses. She introduced herself as Randy Macon or Bacon.

"I know this is hard for you," she said, unruffled by Lyn's remarks. "That's why you're getting this door-to-door service, to try and make it easier."

Lyn replied, "You don't need to worry. I'd have shown up. I have nothing to hide."

During the trip to Mineola, Randy chatted pleasantly about irrelevant matters. Lyn said little. She felt wrung out and, at the same time, charged with nervousness. She chain-smoked.

How dare they expect her to testify against him?

When they reached the courthouse, Randy looked at her watch. They would have a while to wait, she said, and suggested a cup of coffee.

Lyn did not want coffee, but managed to eat a Danish pastry, then lit another cigarette. She ordered a glass of water to wet her mouth.

"What sort of case do they have?" she demanded. "I mean, why do they think it was Owen? He respected Ruth, he really did. They were talking about a divorce, but he still liked her as a person. He'd never go at her like that. It's just—" *Incredible. Ridiculous.* No word seemed adequate.

"Well, you know," Randy explained, "it's already been mentioned at the trial, so it doesn't matter if I say it, but there are some things that are generally true, and others that just don't wash. Like the burglar idea. I mean, nobody's ruling it out, but the police have had experience, and they know most burglars wouldn't go into a house in daylight. They want the darkness. Most house burglars aren't armed, and their usual instinct is to run. Even if they're caught, they'd rather be caught for breaking and entering than for murder."

Lyn's hands felt numb. Slowly she lowered the cigarette from her lips.

"That's the stupidest thing I ever heard. It's just not logical that a burglar would break in at night when everybody's there."

"According to police statistics," Randy argued, "that's mostly when they do break in, unless they happen to know the family's away. It's less risky."

Lyn drew again on the cigarette. Not only her hands but her arms had gone numb.

"So?" she responded after a moment. "You're trying an individual case, not a police statistic. Didn't you ever hear of anybody being desperate? A junkie, or something? You're in a blind alley, friend."

Randy said nothing. Lyn wondered if this had been a plan to break her down, undermine her confidence. Had Randy any right to discuss the case with her?

But she had not been discussing the case. She had been discussing burglars, which, according to her, had nothing to do with the case.

When Randy did speak, it was to say, "I suppose we'd better get on over there." She watched solicitously as Lyn stood up. "Are you all right?"

"I'm fine." Lyn was disembodied, floating. They got into the car and drove to the courthouse complex. The parking lot was crowded. She wondered how many of those cars were for Owen's trial, how many people had come to watch.

They mounted a flight of steps to a pair of huge glass doors. She could see right through the building to the doors on the other side, and there were people—

A flashbulb blazed. A hand, clutching a microphone, reached for her face. Voices battered her.

"Are you testifying for the prosecution, Mrs. Singleton?"

"What do you plan to do when this is over?"

She wavered on her feet. Randy took her elbow and tried to hurry her away. "You don't have to talk to them."

The reporters followed. Lyn was surprised that they had recognized her, or known who she was. She found her hand trembling as she lit another cigarette. Before she could finish it, they called her into the courtroom.

She walked past an endless stretch of faces, all turned to look at her. She kept her eyes straight ahead, searching for Owen, and finally found him. She had not seen him since the trial began. He was wearing his gray suit with the maroon and gray striped tie. She knew all his clothes. She knew everything about him. As their eyes met, she saw a crease appear in his cheek, and knew that he was smiling just for her.

Some of the knots inside her loosened. At least he was not letting it get him down.

They swore her in and then there was a long wait. Like a football game, she thought. Long, long waits.

Finally a man walked toward her, gray-haired and solemn, and the questioning began.

"Mrs. Singleton, how long have you known the defendant?"

"Uh—about a year and a half."

"What were the circumstances of your first meeting?"

"I went to work in his office. As a secretary." She realized that her whole personal life would be uncovered before these strangers. And she would tell all of it. Not hide a thing. Not one single thing.

"Did you ever see the defendant socially?"

She nodded and moved her mouth.

"Louder, please. When was the first time you saw the defendant socially?"

"What do you mean socially?"

The prosecutor looked annoyed. "After working hours, for any reason not connected with work."

She considered for a moment. "I don't know. I guess—a couple of weeks after I went there. We had—I think we had lunch."

It sounded reasonable, but that, she knew, would not be the end of it.

Gradually it came out: the evenings, the weekends, even the nights in Tim Brandon's apartment. She wondered if Tim

Brandon was there among the spectators. She had no idea what he looked like.

That alone made her feel ashamed. They had made love in Ruth's father's apartment, betraying his daughter, and now she was dead.

"On any of those occasions, did you have intimate relations with the defendant?"

"On most of them, yes." Her voice dropped. Again they told her to speak up.

"Did you and the defendant at any time discuss plans to be married?"

"Oh, yes. Sometimes. But he couldn't—"

"Just answer the question, please."

"That's part of my answer."

She was not allowed to give it. She saw what was happening. He would edit her statements to make them as damning as possible. Perhaps the defense attorney would bring out about the buildings, and how Owen was trying to sell them one by one, to disentangle his finances from Ruth's.

She hoped the prosecutor would ask her about the murder morning. He did not. He only painted her as a scheming marriage wrecker, an adventuress for whose favors a man had killed his blameless wife.

She had guessed it would be like that. She did not flinch, even knowing the press was taking it all down, even when she almost began to see herself as they portrayed her.

The court was adjourned for lunch. Again Randy took her in hand. She pictured Randy as a keeper, a guard, more than anything else.

In the afternoon, the interrogation resumed. She did not know how many hours it lasted. She dared not look at her watch.

Please, please, she begged the defense attorney silently. *Don't skip cross-questioning.*

"Your witness," said the prosecution.

The defense attorney rose.

He was longer and leaner than the prosecutor. In some ways, he was an echo of Owen. There were others at the table with Owen, a younger man and a woman. A whole battery of defense attorneys.

He took her back over the same ground covered by the prosecutor, but skillfully made their love more innocent. It was a force of destiny which neither could control. He emphasized her marriage, her effort to spare herself and Owen further agony. He did not ask her what Owen had said about her marriage.

He brought her to the evening of November fifth. He asked about her errand. Probably he had gotten that from the police. Did he know how relevant it was?

Please, please.

"What time did you arrive in the office on the morning of November sixth?"

"Between eleven-thirty and twelve. I don't know the exact time."

"Was Mr. Holdridge in the office when you arrived?"

"No, he was with me. We came in together."

"Where did you meet Mr. Holdridge that morning?"

"At my apartment."

A gasp went around the courtroom. She looked at Owen. His eyes seemed to burn, but she could not read his expression. She turned away quickly.

"What time did the defendant arrive at your apartment?"

"At eight o'clock. He phoned beforehand."

"Objection!"

She did not understand what the prosecutor objected to.

Again, the questions. They led her back over the entire morning, minute by minute. Owen's phone call to her, the instant coffee, even the intimate relations. His call to Ruth. She herself had heard Ruth's voice. Yes, she recognized it, she had talked to Ruth before.

And then their ride into the city, their visit to the notary public, and their stop on Nineteenth Street to deliver the papers.

"To what address did you deliver those papers?"

"I don't remember," she said. "I waited in the car because we couldn't park, and he took them in."

"Do you remember the buliding?"

"Uh—not really. Just the street. There were a lot of warehouses and trucks. He told me to drive around the block if I had to, and I was looking to see if a policeman came, or if I was in the way."

"How long did you wait in the car?"

"A couple of minutes. It wasn't long. Then he came back."

"What did you do then?"

"We drove back uptown. Parked the car in a garage. Then we stopped for coffee, and then we went to the office."

"Did you enter the office together?"

"Yes, we did. I didn't want to, because I was afraid—"

"Objection!"

"Just answer the question, please. Did anyone see you enter the office?"

"Yes. Doris Peltzer. She's our bookkeeper."

The defense attorney questioned her minutely, bringing out every detail of the morning. She saw the prosecutor taking notes. They would go at her now and try to destroy her. She had never seen a real trial before, but she knew about them from television. She knew how savage they could be.

"Has anyone ever questioned you before about the morning of November sixth?"

"Yes. The police."

"What did you tell the police?"

"I told them—that I was alone that morning. That I delivered the papers myself."

"Was that the truth?"

"No."

"Why did you lie to the police?"

"Mr. Holdridge asked me to. He thought—"

"Objection!"

The defense eyed her sternly. "You don't know what Mr. Holdridge thought. Tell the court what he *said.*"

"I . . . don't . . ." She struggled to remember. "He said if nobody knew I was with him that morning, not to tell them. He said they might assume he spent the night with me."

There was a whispered conference, and she was told to step down. She glanced at the prosecutor. She had been so sure—

The trial should have ended there, she thought, after her testimony. They would throw the whole thing out of court.

But she was wrong. They called her again the next day. Now it was the prosecutor's turn.

It was as bad as she had expected. The previous day, she had been his witness. He had treated her with relative courtesy, his only desire being to prove that Owen had a lover. Now, suddenly, she had become the enemy.

He ripped into her memory first. "Didn't this really happen on another day, and not the morning of November sixth?"

"No, it was November sixth. It was the same day he got the news that something happened to his wife."

"When he asked you to telephone his wife from your apartment, did he want you to dial the call for him?"

"He said to get her on the phone, and then he'd talk to her."

"Did he ever ask you to do that before? To get his wife on the phone?"

"Sometimes."

"Didn't he usually dial the calls himself?"

"Not always. Not if he was busy."

"On the morning of November sixth when the call was made, you were not at the office. Didn't you wonder why he asked you to dial the call that time?"

"Well, he was in the bathroom, getting dressed."

"Didn't you think it was strange that he asked you to call his wife from your apartment?"

"Objection!"

The objection was overruled. She was forced to answer. "I did at first, but he said—"

"Mightn't it have been for the purpose of establishing that Ruth Holdridge was alive and well at nine A.M., to provide an alibi for the man who engineered her death?"

"Objection, Your Honor. That is pure conjecture and has no place in a court of law."

"Objection sustained. The jury will disregard the state's remark."

She tried to speak. "He was worried about her." This time the prosecutor interrupted. The subject was closed—after the state had made sure that the jury absorbed this latest possibility.

She was helpless. She felt the heat of anger radiating through her body, but could do nothing about it.

The prosecutor continued to question her. How had the defendant behaved that morning?

As usual, of course. She did not mention that he seemed on edge after they reached the office. That he frequently looked at his watch. It was because he had a luncheon appointment, but they would find another reason. Why, Ruth had planned to come in the next day to sign over one of the buildings. There was no need for him to kill her.

She was dismissed and the trial went on. A household insurance company told about some pieces of jewelry that were missing. Score a weak one for the defense. The prosecutor insisted that the disappearance of valuables was very easy to effect.

Then the prosecution brought out the fact that in the last year, Owen Holdridge had bought half a million dollars' worth of life insurance on his wife. Lyn read about it in the newspaper and was ill. Everything seemed to be against him. Everything except her own testimony.

She hated each day she had to spend in the office, away from him. Each day—until the case went to the jury. Then Mr.

Tannen gave her time off so that she could attend. She almost didn't want to. She was afraid to go, but he urged her.

"Owen will need you," he said.

And she thought: My God, I have no more secrets. I'm naked.

Everyone knew now, including her parents, and Beverly and Eddie. She was glad she no longer lived at home. She was only sorry about Eddie. He was too young to understand.

The jury deliberated all that day and was sequestered for the night. She went home to her apartment in Elmhurst. There was no other place where she could be alone. In the morning she rode back on the Long Island Railroad, and was in Mineola by nine o'clock.

Another long wait. Hours of deliberation. Randy Macon or Bacon told her it was a good sign.

She did not know if it was good. She waited outside, sitting on a bench next to the courthouse in the hot June sunshine. It was three o'clock. She was aware that someone snapped her picture. Another reporter. She did not care.

She lifted her head, sensing a rush of activity. She saw people hurrying inside, and went inside herself. More flashbulbs popped as she fought her way to the courtroom.

It seemed an eternity before the jury filed in. She found herself trembling, and held her arms to steady them. She tried to imagine the worst—leaving the courtroom alone, with all those reporters asking her how she felt.

The court was called to order and the jury questioned. The foreman stood up, a small man in his fifties, wearing a green plaid jacket.

"Your Honor, we find the defendant not guilty."

She stared through a haze, hardly daring to believe it. She barely moved, and felt the woman beside her watching her. She heard fragments of speech. ". . . death caused by person or persons unknown."

When the court was dismissed, she rose and stood buffeted in the aisle. Someone said, "Congratulations." A man was smirking at her. Only then did she realize that some people would never believe the verdict.

She waited, but Owen did not come toward her. He was talking with his attorneys. She began to understand that he could not come to her yet. She would have to leave by herself in any case, and maybe it was all over.

But at least he was free.

She joined the crowd that oozed out of the courtroom, and did not hear the reporters who badgered her with questions. But this time when the cameras flashed, there was a small, private smile on her face.

14

Not long after the end of the trial, she met his children for the first time. He arranged to have them brought into the city for a visit to his office.

He escorted them from desk to desk, introducing them, two solemn, brown-eyed children, so different from each other. The boy, Dennis, still a child, was clearly uninterested in meeting the women who worked for his father. He wanted to get on with lunch.

For Tina, it was different. Her mind reached out in awareness, remembering the trial. The trial. She stared long and hard at Lyn, the woman whom her father had loved when he should have loved her mother. The woman who was alive when her mother was dead.

Lyn said, "It's nice to meet you, Tina. I haven't seen you before. Is this your first trip to the office?"

"No," replied Tina. A cool reminder that her mother had once existed.

"I hope you enjoy your visit."

It seemed rude to turn back to her typewriter while the girl stood and watched her, although clearly the conversation was at an end. Tina was too old for the blatant stare of early childhood. She did it deliberately. It lasted for a minute or two, until the children were led away.

Soon Lyn and Owen began dating again—gradually, at first,

playing it in low key for any reporter who might still hover, waiting to pounce.

Finally the time came when she was invited to Great Harbor for Sunday dinner.

"Is your daughter going to be there?" she asked.

"Of course. Why not? What's the matter?"

I don't think she likes me."

"She just feels a little awkward. She'll get used to you. That's why I want you to come."

It was more than awkwardness, but Lyn could not describe it to the child's father.

"Look," he said, "this present situation is no damn good. I want to be with you and I want to be with the kids, too. The only way I can manage both is to marry you as soon as possible, but I have to get them used to the idea first."

"Won't it look bad? she asked.

"What will? Getting married? If people want to see it that way, I can't help it. There's nothing they can do, anyway."

Which was true. And it was nearly a year since Ruth had been killed.

On Sunday she took a train to Great Harbor, where Owen met her at the station. His live-in housekeeper was away for the weekend. Owen cooked the dinner himself and kept up a lively conversation while Dennis was quietly shy and Tina hostile.

Lyn could not meet Owen's liveliness, but she tried to be warm and loving toward the children. It was not easy. She could imagine how they felt. What else might she expect—she who had been the alleged reason in the prosecution's case against their father? But her testimony had acquitted him. Didn't she get any points for that? She supposed not. They were too young to realize what it had meant for her to make those admissions.

Not that it mattered in the long run. She would have been dragged through the mud in any case, despite his gallant efforts to protect her.

She looked around the table and saw Tina watching her. She must stop thinking about the trial. It probably showed on her face. She turned to Dennis and asked brightly, "Do you like basketball? I have a brother who plays basketball. Maybe you can get together with him sometime."

After her visit that day, Owen informed the children that he intended to marry her.

He did not tell her what their reaction was. She could only guess. And she, as well as they, knew that she would never be able to fill their mother's place.

They were married in the middle of October. They honeymooned for a weekend at the Catskill hotel where they had gone once before, and returned to Great Harbor on Sunday night.

"I wish," she said as his car pushed its way up the steep driveway, "we could live somewhere else. It would be easier for the children, too."

"But this is my home." He sounded surprised.

"I know. And it was her home, too. You can't forget that, can you?"

"Life must go on. It's also the children's home. They're used to it."

She did not answer. He had no intention of moving, she could see that.

The only time she had been inside the house was that day she came to dinner. On a trip to the bathroom, she had seen the master bedroom. It had a double bed. When they set the date for their marriage, she had asked him to change the bed. Now she wondered if he had done it.

He parked in front of the house. A floodlight shone above the garage door, but there did not seem to be any light inside the house.

"Where are they?" she asked.

"The kids? I arranged for them to spend the night with friends. I thought it would be easier that way."

"It is." She felt the fibers of her body relax, knowing she did not have to face the children yet. "But what about tomorrow? Will they be coming home from school—here?" She thought of Tina coming home a year ago to find her mother's battered body.

"I'll be here. I'm taking tomorrow off."

"Oh, thank you, Owen." She put her arms around his neck just as he unlocked the front door. He picked her up and carried her inside. She had not meant for him to do that. She only meant to thank him.

He set her down, and she stood alone while he closed the door and turned on the lights. The house felt empty and chilly. It was almost as though Ruth's ghost were there. She did not believe in ghosts, but she believed in this. Ruth would never have wanted her in that place.

She shuddered. He turned up the thermostat. "It'll warm up in a few minutes," he said.

With the lights on, the drapes closed, and the oil burner working, it did begin to feel warmer. She took off her coat and put it over a chair.

"Uh-uh," he said as he hung it on a hanger. "You live here now."

"It's going to take me a while to get used to it," she admitted. "What did you do about the bed?"

"It's a new bed. Don't worry about that."

She felt relieved. It would still be the same room, but at least she would not have to sleep in Ruth's bed.

They had stopped for dinner on the way home. There was nothing to do now but love each other, which they did.

"I can't believe we're married," she sighed from his arms, "after all this. It's been two years."

"What's been two years?" he murmured sleepily. They lay under sheets and blankets that she hoped were also new, but she dared not ask, for fear of learning that they weren't.

"Since we met each other. Don't you remember? I never thought I'd end up marrying you. I mean, at first."

"I thought we were always here, you and I. Right here, like this." He seemed to be dropping off. She was wide awake.

"Do you ever think of her?" she asked.

He stirred, perhaps impatiently. "Sometimes. We had a lot of years together. Why?"

"I just wondered. I can't help thinking about her. It's her house, her children . . ."

"And your husband." He rose onto his elbow. "I've heard of jealous second wives. You're not going to be like that, are you?"

"I'm not jealous. It's not that. But she did live here. It's not going to be easy with the children, is it?"

"No," he agreed. "Probably not."

When the children arrived home from school the next day, they found her waiting beside their father to welcome them. Dennis came first. He hugged his father, and when she reached for him, he pulled back shyly and murmured, "Hello," then scurried away to his room.

Tina was late. Although her school let out at three o'clock, she did not come home until four-thirty. They saw her dragging slowly up the driveway. Against her better judgment, Lyn opened the door for her. At that, Tina stopped short and stared through narrowed eyes.

Owen asked from the doorway, "Do you always get home this late? What happened?"

"I missed the bus," Tina answered in a voice that carried a note of triumph.

"And you walked? Why didn't you call? I'd have come for you."

"I felt like walking." She tried to push past them. She was caught by Owen who embraced her stiff body and let her go. Then she, too, hurried away without acknowledging Lyn's presence.

The next time the children appeared was at dinner. There the pattern seemed to jell. Dennis's attitude was mostly one of awkwardness, but he could be drawn into conversation. Tina maintained an elaborate charade that ignored Lyn's existence completely. When Lyn spoke to her, she did not hear. She would ask someone else to pass the salt or the butter, even when it was closest to Lyn. She talked to her father and brother, but Lyn remained part of the air in the room.

At the end of the meal, under Owen's directive, Tina helped clear the table. Even though they were working together, she managed to ignore her new stepmother.

Lyn was exhausted. She hoped Tina was, too. "How long can she keep this up?" she asked Owen, who had come to the kitchen to show her how to load the dishwasher.

"I'd hate to guess, but I wouldn't worry about it. She'll get used to you. It'll blow over in time. You'll notice I'm not trying to present you as a new mother for them. You're just Lyn."

She had noticed, and she thought it was wise. The brutal manner in which they had lost their own mother would make it especially hard for anyone to substitute for her.

The next day Owen returned to work and Lyn was alone in the house when the children came home. Dennis was obviously eager to establish a new normality in his life. He allowed Lyn to converse with him and ask him about his day, even to make him a peanut butter sandwich. Tina's manner had not changed. She was sunny and bright with her brother, but coldly oblivious to Lyn.

As the days went by, Lyn developed a real fondness for Dennis. He was her brother Eddie, the member of her own family whom she loved best.

"I always feel that kids deserve a better break than what they get," she confided to Owen on Saturday evening, after their first entire day spent as a family.

"What do you mean? My kids have always had everything. The only thing wrong is what happened to Ruth."

"I don't mean material things. I just mean—well, maybe I remember being a kid better than you do. It's really hard."

Her sympathy went no farther than Dennis. She tried to feel for Tina, too, but Tina frightened her. The child's hostility was

monstrous and palpable, something that seemed to have no
end and no solution. For week after week it went on, with Tina
living, talking, acting and reacting as though Lyn were not
there. Lyn tried to behave naturally, to maintain a pretense
that their relationship was normal, to address Tina whenever
an occasion arose, and not mind that she did not answer. But it
was wearing her down.

"Talk to her, Owen," she pleaded. Christmas was coming.
She could not bear to have their first Christmas ruined in this
way.

"I've talked to her a million times," he said. "She won't even
discuss it."

"How can she not discuss it, if you ask her about it?"

He seemed reluctant to answer. "She says she doesn't know
what I mean."

"Owen, she's a child. You *must* be able to deal with her."

He hesitated, then replied, "I don't know. Sometimes she
doesn't seem like a child at all."

Midway through December, the weather turned cold and
snow began to fall. It started as a few flakes when the children
were leaving for school. Dennis gave a whoop of excitement.
Lyn tried to prepare him for the fact that the first snowfall
rarely amounted to anything.

She had guessed wrong. The morning remained dark and
gloomy and snow continued to fall. She stood at a window,
alone in the house, and watched it pile on the lawn and the
driveway.

School was dismissed two hours early. The children came
home and played outside in the snow. She thought of Owen,
who fortunately had taken a train to work, although even the
trains could be thrown off by bad weather.

During the afternoon the temperature warmed enough so
that the snow changed to freezing rain. She telephoned Owen,
suggesting that he leave work early.

"I'll be all right," he said. "How is it out there? Maybe it'll melt by evening."

"It won't. It's getting all covered with ice. Everything's slippery."

"I'll check with you before I leave. And don't worry, I can take a taxi from the station. I'll just leave my car there if I have to."

She wanted him at home. She felt alone and frightened, although the weather was not really a threat. What she did not like was being shut in with the children, with that terrible girl, in weather that seemed opaque and impenetrable. It was as though they were locked away from all help.

Dusk fell early, giving a last glimpse of nature's treacherous beauty. Every branch, every twig, every telephone wire was encased in hard, glittering ice. The roads and walks were slick and deadly.

Perhaps Owen would not be able to come home at all. She could not bear that. She tried to put it from her mind and concentrate on preparing dinner.

After a while she called his office again. No one answered. It must have meant he was on his way. Unless he had already gone to a hotel to spend the night.

She was making Salisbury steak with a ring of mashed potatoes. The children liked it, but they would not want to sit down to dinner with her alone. At least Tina wouldn't, and it would be a terrible strain for little Dennis to have to talk with each of them separately.

The telephone rang. *Owen,* she thought, quickly washing the hamburger grease from her hands and picking up the phone in its corner of the dining room.

The room was dark. Through the windows she could see the icy whiteness outside.

"Help me!" said a man's voice. "She fell downstairs. She might be dead. Come quick!"

Owen? Was it Owen? It sounded very like him. Goosebumps prickled her skin.

"Where—are you?" Her mouth felt dry and heavy.

"Where do you think? Come quick, she hurt herself bad."

Her head reeled. She wanted to say she couldn't come, the roads were all icy, but the phone clicked in her ear.

Who did he mean? *Who* was hurt badly? Ruth was already dead.

The voice had been urgent. Desperate. She put on her coat, but could not find her boots. From the den, which had been built as a maid's room off the kitchen, came the sound of television. She would be gone only a minute. *Where am I supposed to go?*

Somehow she knew she had to go home. The voice on the telephone had been her father.

She motioned to Dennis.

"I've got to go out," she told him. "Something's happened to my parents. You'll be all right, Tina's old enough. And your daddy will be home soon."

She oughtn't to leave them alone on a night like this. But her mother might be dying. Dennis stared after her, still absorbing what she had told him, as she hurried into the garage.

The garage door worked by remote control. She did not even think of the condition of the roads as she eased the car out into crunchy snow and ice.

She was all mixed up. Her mother? Her father? But she had thought it was Owen. She remembered so clearly that time they telephoned him about Ruth.

Something's happened, was all he told her then. *An emergency.*

Just outside the garage, the car ran over a bump. She caught her breath and began to tremble. She had driven over something. She felt sick.

The ground was slippery under her wheels as she moved forward a few more feet and looked back. In the red glow of the taillights, she saw it. Something lumpy in the snow. Something long and—

No. It can't be.

It was exactly the form of a human being. She felt that it was Ruth Holdridge.

Ruth. She had driven over Ruth.

Without thinking, she stepped on the gas pedal to get away. The car slipped to one side of the road and then the other.

"Stop!" she screamed. It spun in a quarter circle. She saw the edge of the hill. She put her hands over her ears and knew this was the end.

15

I must have been crazy, she thought as she lay in bed after the accident. Crazy to think that was Ruth.

It had been nothing but a ridge of snow fallen from the roof. She realized that later. She never told anyone that she had thought it was Ruth.

Her injuries were relatively minor. Two cracked ribs and a bump on the head. She was lucky, Owen kept telling her. Lucky even to be alive, going out on a night like that.

The next day her father came to visit her. He brought her a box of chocolates. It was his way of atoning.

"Didn't mean to get you all upset," he told her gruffly. She could see that he thought the fault was largely hers.

"She fell down the stairs, all the way down," he went on. "She didn't move. I got scared. I tried to call Beverly but I couldn't get her."

Of course he had tried to call Beverly first. She lived closer, only a few blocks away. But Beverly had gone to pick up her children at a birthday party, and had stayed for a cup of coffee.

All those stupid, stupid little things, Lyn thought. That chain of events. And she herself might have died.

But only because she had panicked, thinking of Ruth, and that was probably due to her own feelings of guilt for trying to take Ruth's place.

Her mother was better now, he told her. She had only been

knocked unconscious by the fall. Finally he had thought of calling an ambulance, but long before it came, Mom had revived.

After he left, she lay with her eyes closed, wondering how she could have thought it was Owen's voice. But there was a similarity. That was the odd part about it. And she had expected the caller to be Owen.

That afternoon she woke from a half doze to find Tina coming into the room.

Her eyes opened with a start, all vestiges of sleep falling away. This was the first time Tina had ever sought her out.

Lyn struggled to sit up, rearranging her pillows. "Hello, dear. It's nice to see you."

The words sounded stupid and empty, but she was flustered and did not know what else to say.

Tina stopped near the foot of the bed. She stood looking at Lyn, her mouth tight and sullen. It was a familiar expression. Gone was the smiling pixie in the photograph on Owen's desk.

"Would you like a chocolate?" Lyn asked, reaching for the box. "My father brought them. I guess he felt sorry, since he was the one who made that silly phone call that sent me rushing out into the snow."

Tina did not move or speak. Lyn set down the candy box, adding unnecessarily, "You can have one, if you like."

Tina continued to stare. Lyn reached for her cigarettes, grateful that there was something she could do. As she lit one, Tina turned and walked out of the room.

Lyn took a long drag on her cigarette and then lay back, slowly exhaling. She thought of the two children whose mother had been murdered and their father accused of the crime. Most people could spend an entire lifetime without having to go through such an ordeal, and to young children, it must have seemed as though the earth had dropped away. She ought to pity Tina—and God, how she tried.

When Owen came home that evening, she told him of the episode with his daughter.

"She came in here as if she wanted to talk, and then she didn't say anything. She just stared. It bothered me."

"Maybe she really did want to talk. Tell you she's sorry," Owen conjectured. "And then she couldn't get up her nerve. It takes a lot of nerve to apologize, you know."

"I'm not sure what she wanted. And I don't know if she knew, either."

The following day she heard Tina coming down the hall, and was better prepared for her visit.

"Well, hello," Lyn said. Tina regarded her calmly and again sauntered to the foot of the bed.

"I still have these chocolates." Lyn uncovered the box. "Why don't you take a handful for you and Dennis?"

Tina folded her arms and stared.

Lyn was about to resort to another cigarette, when Tina spoke.

"Are you glad my mother's dead?"

The hand, poised above the cigarette pack, stopped and slowly withdrew.

"Of course not. Why would I be glad?"

She wished she had not asked. She wished she had gone ahead and taken the cigarette.

"Because if my mother were alive, you couldn't marry my father."

I'm dealing with a child, Lyn reminded herself. She's only a child, and she's badly hurt.

"Tina, I know how you feel. It's a terrible thing to lose your mother, but nobody wished her dead. You've got to believe that."

She was saying it badly. Tina moved forward until her knees were pressed against the bed.

"That's stupid. She's dead and somebody killed her, so obviously somebody wished her dead. And I think it was you."

She stood back to watch the effect. Lyn's hand went out automatically for the cigarettes.

"I understand how you must feel about me, Tina, but that's just not logical. Probably even the burglar who—"

"It wasn't any burglar." Tina's voice overrode her own. "You know what it was. Somebody got paid to kill my mother, and someday—I wish it would happen to you."

With that, she was gone.

The first words she ever spoke to me, thought Lyn.

It was horrible. It was what they had suggested about Owen, and he was acquitted. Was that where Tina had gotten the idea?

She was glad when she heard Owen's car that night. She was glad it was Friday and he would be home for the weekend.

He came cheerily into the bedroom. "How are you feeling, baby? How was your day?"

"Terrible. Owen, I don't know what to do."

"Why? What happened?"

"Tina. I know how she feels, but does it have to be like this?" She told him what the girl had said to her. When she finished, he sat down on the bed and took her in his arms.

She found her face wet with tears against his shoulder.

"Where did she get an idea like that? Tell me."

He shook his head. "We're going to have to work something out."

"But what? Maybe I should go away for a while."

"That's ridiculous. Why should you?"

"Maybe it's partly the shock—you know, when she found her mother. Do you think it would help to try some kind of counseling? Maybe if she just had someone to talk to."

"I don't know." He swallowed perceptibly. "I'm afraid she'd be insulted at the very idea."

"But it's not anything—"

"I don't want to try it right now, okay? Let's just let things go for a while. She'll have to come off this eventually."

"I don't know. Maybe I'll break first. I'm pretty near it already."

He laughed and gave her shoulder a playful shake, forgetting about the cracked ribs. "Buck up, kid. You've got more spunk than that. I'll talk to her."

"I liked it better when she wasn't even speaking to me. It would suit her, wouldn't it, to think I'd do a thing like that?"

"You know kids. Big imagination. There's something else, too."

She waited, holding his arm with both of hers.

He said, "You know the thief stole some things, some jewelry and stuff."

"The killer."

"All right, the killer. I couldn't remember everything we had, especially Ruth's stuff, but I listed what I could, and the insurance company paid. But just the other day a couple of those things turned up."

"When? You didn't tell me."

"I didn't want to bother you. It was right after your accident. You were at the hospital getting X-rayed. Tina found a couple of things, a pin and a pair of earrings. Might have been right here in this room. I can't remember."

"How can you not remember?"

He sighed, rubbing his forehead. "It doesn't matter. They probably got misplaced and I thought they were stolen. I've already notified the insurance company."

"But it does matter. I've lived in this house for two months. In this room. She knows it. *I've* never seen those things."

"As I said, Ruth probably mislaid them. Don't get yourself worked up. Tina found them and I suppose it pleased her to think it had something to do with you."

"What was she doing—"

"I don't know what she was doing. But it's her home. There's nothing off limits to her, is there?"

That was not the point. She not only wanted to know what Tina had been doing in her room, but what Tina had been doing there *then*, just after her accident. Like a vulture. She felt something cold beginning to grow, reaching out with tentacles to swallow her. She did not know what it was. She could not think what it meant. It could have been many things.

He changed his clothes and went to warm up the TV dinners. She lit a cigarette, but quickly put it out. She found she was having trouble breathing. It was as though she were suffocating, and not only because her chest was taped and in pain.

Probably he was right. Probably Ruth had mislaid some of her jewelry, taken it off after a late party and then forgotten it.

Or maybe the burglar had stashed it somewhere when Ruth surprised him in the room.

Whatever the answer, it still frightened her that Tina had been snooping. There had been a whole year after Ruth's death before Lyn came into the household, when it would have made sense for the girl to be poring through her mother's things.

She closed her eyes, remembering the silly daydreams she had once had of her life with Owen. Now it was all spoiled, because of that girl. Even if she had children of her own—and that might be in about eight months. She had reason to believe she was pregnant, but did not want to count on it.

And now a new dread. If she were to have a baby, how would Tina react? What would she do?

As it turned out, she did not have to worry much longer about Tina. Soon after the Christmas holidays, Tina reached the limit of her tolerance, and left home.

It was not her father whom she wished to escape. She considered him merely misguided, and besides, he was her father. Lyn must pay the penalty for everything that had happened. As Lyn paid no penalty, Tina felt betrayed, and moved to the home of a friend whose parents agreed to take her in as a surrogate sister for their only child. Against their protests, Owen insisted upon paying them a monthly sum for her keep.

Dennis missed his sister, but he seemed relieved to have the tension gone. Tina had tried to turn him against Lyn, and he needed to accept his new stepmother. He needed peace and security.

For the first time, Lyn felt as though she were really living in her own home. She felt it all the more with her discovery that she was indeed pregnant.

"Jesus," said Owen when she told him her news, "you could have lost it in that stupid accident. Will you do me a favor and take care of yourself from now on?" The rough words were softened when he held and kissed her.

Although he never mentioned it, she knew Owen entertained a hope that Tina would someday return to the expanded family. It was expanded by two, for on the third of August, Lyn gave birth to twin boys.

Tina did not return. She visited from time to time, but she could not fully accept her new brothers. Lyn hated to see Owen hurt. Once again she proposed that they try to find some help for the girl.

He shook his head. He was slumped on the sofa after one of Tina's visits, his legs straight out in front of him, his head bowed. Lyn thought she had never seen him look so unhappy.

"Why not?" she asked. "Think how miserable she must be, carrying around all that hatred. And look what it's doing to you."

"I'm surviving," he said. "In the first place, you couldn't ever get her to see anybody. She thinks she's perfectly all right and we're the ones who are wrong. You can't force a person to get help when they don't want it. In the second place, you know what it would do to her to have all that dragged up again. Remember, she was the one who—"

"I remember. But it wouldn't just be dragging it up. It would be helping her get over it. That's probably a big part of why she feels the way she does."

Again he shook his head. "She'd have to relive the whole thing."

"Owen, she's not going to forget it. You know that. But she shouldn't have to keep it to herself."

He held up his hand, waving it back and forth as though to quiet her.

"No argument, darling. I know what's best for my own kid. I know her personality."

She sighed. "I don't agree with you, but what can I do?"

"Nothing. So we'll just leave it at that, okay?" He patted the sofa beside him. "Come here, little mother."

She smiled and nestled against him, basking in his love and approval, and sharing his pride. She could not help thinking it had been rather cute of her to produce identical twins. Her parents were thrilled by the babies and by her good marriage. She had everything she could have wanted. Everything but the acceptance of her stepdaughter.

16

The bright sky had disappeared. It was gray outside, but not yet evening. Gray with clouds. A rain sky. Or snow. She felt ridiculous, not knowing what time of year it was.

She was in a hospital. That confused her, for the only time she had ever been in a hospital was when the twins were born.

She thought some time had passed since then, but maybe she only imagined it. She was dreaming that Tina had left home, that she and Owen had twin boys and were living a happy life together.

How could it be imagination? She even had names for the twins. Neal and Paul. She knew what they looked like. They were boys, no longer babies. How could none of it be real?

But it was very bewildering. And maybe she only wanted it to be real. Wanted it so badly that she thought it *was* real. Wanted Tina out of the way.

A chill went through her when she thought of Tina.

The man she had seen with the mask on his face and the winged eyebrows—he was Danger. Tina wanted her to die as Ruth had died, and the man—She knew that if he got into the room, Tina's wish would come true.

She felt vulnerable, lying alone and helpless. She remembered that she could raise her bed. But the button was on the right side, and her right hand was in a cast. And she couldn't turn to use her left hand without hurting her broken ribs.

She needed a cigarette. Could she reach the pack on her night table?

Something showered against the window. She turned her head, surprised to find that she could move more easily now. She saw drops. It was raining.

She turned again at the sound of footsteps in the corridor. Not stealthy this time. A flash of white—

It was the doctor, trailed by a nurse. Before she could allow herself to feel relief, she studied their eyebrows. The nurse's were blond, the doctor's heavy with tiny, unruly hairs, not smooth and sleek like the winged ones she had seen above the mask.

"How's it going?" he asked. "You're looking much better. How's the mouth?"

She tried to make her lips form a word, but could not think of any word at the moment. She did not know how she felt.

"Still stiff?" He pulled over the chair and sat looking at her with intense dark eyes. She felt embarrassed at being studied. What was he thinking? Was she only an object, a blob in bandages, or did he see her as a woman? Not a pretty one, certainly, not now, but did he see that she had been pretty before it happened?

"I'm going to try taking some of that stuff off your face," he said. "I don't think you need so much wrapping any more."

With that, he peeled a strip of adhesive tape from near her hairline. She winced, but the discomfort was minor compared with the pain of her injuries.

When he had removed some of the bandages, he peered closely at her face and remarked, "Still discolored, but the laceration's healing nicely."

She cringed. *Why does he have to see me like this?*

His finger traced a line in the air just above her forehead. "Your skin was split right along here, but it's healing well. I don't think there'll be much of a scar, and you can wear your hair over it."

She wanted to ask about the rest of her face. She touched

both cheeks with her left hand. He waited, apparently realizing that she was trying to communicate. Her mouth formed the word "This?"

He smiled delightedly. "He-e-ey, she talks. That's wonderful. This part's just bruised. It'll clear up in time. And that split on your lip will heal. Nobody will even notice it."

After he left, she lay watching the rain against the window, and wondering what she looked like. Bruised, with gashes on her lip and forehead. Owen would come that evening and he would see her. She could imagine the mayhem on her face, the bruises turning green.

She closed her eyes, then opened them, recalling the earlier hospital stay. She remembered that there was a mirror. The table that slid across the bed—the center part was a hinged lid and it had a mirror on the inside.

If she could see herself, she might know who she was. Or maybe she would see a stranger. Maybe she would not recognize herself behind the bruises and lacerations.

It became a compulsion—to see herself. She had to know. She tried to sit up without twisting her torso. If only the button that raised the bed were on the left side instead of the right. The table was on her left, so that she could feed herself, but they had pushed it out of the way after lunch.

She could ring for a nurse. But it seemed too trivial. She did not want to bother the nurses just to push over a table.

She managed to sit up in spite of the pain. It did not hurt as badly as it had the first day. Once she was up, she could swing her legs over the side of the bed. At least her legs had not been broken. She could reach down, slowly, stiffly, in danger of becoming dizzy and falling—and she pressed the button, raising the head of her bed.

She rested for a while after that, but she was pleased with her mobility. It was safer to be able to move. She would not tell anyone she could do it.

She reached forward again, grasped the edge of the table and pulled it toward her. It was on casters and moved easily.

When she had it beside her, she arranged herself back in bed with the sheet over her legs.

Now was the moment. Now she would see herself.

What if it hadn't a mirror? Perhaps not all the tables were so equipped.

Slowly she opened it and groped with her fingers. It was glass. She opened it all the way and stared at the face reflected back at her. The ghastly face with the Frankenstein cut, the straps on her jaw, the puffy eye.

She stared for a long time, not believing. It wasn't possible. Under the straps and the discoloration, she saw a thirty-three-year-old face.

No, she thought. That's not me. It's not me.

She closed the mirror. Lying back on her pillow, she listened to the rain against the window and voices somewhere down the corridor.

She could not understand what had happened. Her memories were out of joint, and they seemed to grow more distant even as she reached for them.

Then, after a while, came the answer. It was soundless, a whisper in her brain.

You are Ruth.

The words slipped through her, icy cold, raising prickles of flesh. They came again.

You are Ruth.

And then she knew.

17

But I'm not Ruth, she thought, gazing at the far wall. *Ruth is dead.*

Another icy shiver. Ruth was going to die. She had seen it all: the affair, the trial, and then their life together after she was gone.

But she was still alive. It hadn't happened yet.

She had seen it through the eyes of the girl. As though she were that girl. The one he loved. It was only wishful thinking that had made her believe she was the loved one instead of herself, the wife he wanted to be rid of.

She was going to die. He wanted her dead. That man in the gauze mask had been sent to kill her.

She turned to look out of the window. It was growing dark. Was this the last time she would ever see the sky?

Tears came into her eyes. One of them rolled across her nose and onto the pillow.

But this was not how Ruth had died. It had happened at home.

How do I know how I'm going to die?

Her head felt dulled, as though she had been thinking too much. She did not know how she knew. She only knew.

It was in the garage. She could not remember, exactly. She had been opening the car door. The next thing she knew, she was in the car and kicking at someone just outside it.

A stranger. With smooth, winged eyebrows.

Somehow she managed to slip past him. He smelled of alcohol. She remembered the smell.

She had ducked away from him and tried to run into the house. He caught her arm, pulled her down, and then he began to hit her. She tried to shield her face, and her hand was smashed.

Then she was in the car again. She felt it moving. She was lying down, looking up through the windshield at the whitish-blue sky. And the car was moving faster and faster.

She tried to sit up. A terrible pain in her chest forced her down. She remembered the hill and how she had gone over it before. She closed her eyes, shutting out the sky, and felt the car hurtle out of control.

And that was all, until she woke up in the hospital.

He hadn't killed her that time. But he knew she was here. He had come to try again.

And again.

It would happen, finally, in her bedroom at home. That was where Ruth had died. In the bedroom. Beaten to death.

So long ago.

I can't be Ruth, she thought. But it's happening to me. The same thing is happening to me.

She heard the sound of dinner carts in the hallway, the clinking of dishes. It would be nice when she could have real food again.

And then she remembered that he had tried to poison her. She would have to be careful. Maybe not eat at all.

But they would feed her through a tube in her nose. She would hate it.

And aide brought in her tray and a cheery greeting. There were two glasses of pink liquid—strawberry—and a cup of broth.

She began with the broth, drinking it slowly. She took everything very slowly. If it were poisoned, the poison would have time to start working before she swallowed too much of it. She was not hungry, and wondered if she would ever be hungry again, lying there in a hospital bed. Although her body still hurt, they had told her that soon she could get up and go to the bathroom. They advised her to take walks, but that would mean going out to the corridor where people would see her face with its ugly bruises. Besides, she might meet someone who knew her, and she would not know that person, even as she didn't know herself.

She finished as much of the liquid as she could endure, with no ill effects. The dishes were still on her table when Owen arrived. He shook out his wet raincoat and hung it over the door.

"All that food?" he joked, seeing her tray. "Watch out you don't get too fat. I don't want to take home a blimp."

He sat down beside her bed in his accustomed chair, stretched out his legs and stared at his foot. For the first time she realized that things between them were not as easy as they had once been. The joke had been clumsy, his jocularity forced.

On his first visit to her here, he had alluded to something—something that had been rough on her, but was over now, according to him. Was this what he meant? Was there someone else?

She put her hand to her jaw and probed the swelling. It was not as painful as it had been in the beginning. She had managed one syllable to the doctor. Perhaps she could try again.

She made her lips shape the sounds carefully. "Owen?"

He raised his head. "You shouldn't be trying to talk!"

"Who am I?"

"Who—" He had half risen from his chair, and now he paused and blinked at her.

"You don't know who you are?" he asked.

She tried to shake her head. The quick motion hurt her neck.

He sat down again, leaning toward her and scrutinizing her face. "How come you know who I am, and you don't know who you are?"

"Please—tell me."

"You're my angel. Of course." The smile-creases appeared in his cheeks. "Who did you think you were?"

"My—name."

The creases vanished. He watched her soberly, apparently realizing the depth of her amnesia.

"Lynette," he said. "Lynette Garrity Holdridge. I could put another name in there."

"No, don't." She had almost forgotten about Joe Singleton.

"Does it mean anything to you? Your name?"

"Yes."

"How much do you remember?"

"Almost everything."

"The accident?"

". . . wasn't an accident." Her mouth was becoming heavier.

"What do you mean?"

She looked at him quickly, moving only her eyes. "How long have I been here?"

"A few days. Since Monday. This is Friday. What do you mean, it wasn't an accident?"

She did not want to go through it and explain the whole thing. He wouldn't believe her. It had happened to Ruth, but he wouldn't believe her.

It happened to Ruth . . .

She could feel her heart, in slow and drumlike beats.

It happened to Ruth . . .

"I wish you'd tell me," he said. His face was clouded, the lines deep. "You didn't do anything to yourself, did you?"

"*No*." Why would she? Because of the trouble he had spoken of? She didn't even know what it was.

"A man." She could barely move her mouth. "A man—beat me."

"*Beat* you?" She saw reflected in his face the horror of Ruth's murder.

"Put me in car."

"I can't believe it. What man? Where was he?"

"Garage."

His forehead rested in his hand. "Baby, baby, I didn't know."

Of course he didn't know. How could he know? She had not been able to tell him until now.

"It's just like Ruth," she said. He looked bleak. She went on, "Same person?"

He took his hand away from his face. "How could it be? Thirteen years ago. It's—" He shook his head. A shudder seemed to run through him. "It's people who come out from the city. They think there's a lot of money in the suburbs. Did you see the man? Get a good look at him?"

"He's here."

"*Here?*"

"Came in my room. I screamed."

"Here? In the hospital?" Owen gave a short, dry laugh. "Baby, you must have been dreaming. A guy like that—"

"Same eyes. Same eyebrows."

"No, darling, a guy like that, a burglar, wouldn't come after you. He'd want to get the hell away as fast as he could."

"I saw him. Tried to kill me."

"But he didn't kill you. Why would he want to make it worse for himself by going after you? Probably you were so upset you thought somebody else—Never mind. Tell me what he looked like. I've got to report this."

"Owen, I'm tired. I'll tell the police."

"I know you're tired, baby. It's easier to tell me, and I'll give them all the information."

"They'll ask me anyway."

"Of course. I forgot. You'd think," he added bitterly, "that I'd have had enough experience with police procedures. But I'll notify them and give them the basics. Now tell me what he looked like."

She thought she had reached the limit of her strength long ago.

"Dark hair."

"Curly? Straight?"

"Smooth. Kind of—smoothed down."

"Hair cream? People don't use hair cream any more."

"No, just smooth. Eyebrows . . ." With her finger, she traced the shape of the man's eyebrows over her own. "Dark eyes. Black."

"Black man? Or black eyes?"

"Black eyes. A white man. Had a—khaki-color jacket. No, a vest. Goosedown vest. Tan."

"Well, which? An army-type jacket?"

"No, vest."

"Everybody has tan goosedown vests."

"Plaid shirt. Flannel."

"Right. I'll call the police as soon as I get home. It's amazing that you remember so much, when he was attacking you."

"Can't forget."

"Of course not. But I mean, it's amazing you saw so much."

She was exhausted. She wished he would leave. Her darling Owen, and she only wanted him out of there so she could rest.

"Like a picture," she said. It was burned into her mind. And yet she had forgotten, for several days. But that, probably, was because of the blows to her head.

He bent down and kissed her. "I'm sorry, baby. I wish I'd known sooner."

She would not tell him that she had forgotten.

After he left, she lay with her eyes closed, listening to the rain on the window.

It must have been the same man. It was too big a coincidence. But why?

She knew how Ruth must have felt.

No, Ruth had died in her attack.

Or had she? Perhaps she had lain there, battered and barely conscious, knowing she would die, and terrified for her children. What would happen to them? Who would take care of them? Who would love them as she did?

Little babies, she thought, her throat tight. Only eleven

years old. They would have their father, but they still needed her.

But I'm not going to die, she remembered. He'll tell the police, and they'll watch, and the man won't dare come again.

After she had rested for a while, she opened the mirror and again studied her face. Puffed and discolored, but she was still Lynette. She looked older, because twelve years had passed since she married Owen.

Twelve years. That was how old Tina had been when she found her mother dead.

Now Tina was twenty-five. They seldom saw her, although she lived not far away, in Larchmont, just across Long Island Sound. Probably she saw Owen more often, for like him, she worked in the city. Lyn imagined them having lunch together, perhaps sometimes with Tina's husband, who was an account executive somewhere. It was all vague, for Lyn had not even attended their wedding, knowing she was not wanted. Sometimes she felt directly responsible for the rift between father and daughter, although the fault was mostly Tina's, but could you really blame a child?

She was not a child any more, yet the child still lived inside her. The child still directed how she thought and felt. It would not be denied.

But there were the other children. Dennis, at Amherst. He had come home for Christmas, but left soon afterward to visit a girlfriend in Boston. And there were Paul and Neal. She would have liked to give Owen another daughter, but Paul and Neal were twins, and that seemed, especially to Owen, to be enough family.

Eleven years old last August. Almost the age Tina had been when—

But they were so young. What if the horror that had happened to Tina should happen to them?

It almost had. If Leigh Elliott hadn't seen her—As Owen said, her car would not have been visible from the road. She would not have been found until Paul and Neal came home from school, walking up the driveway from the bus. And by then, she might well have been dead from her injuries.

Where had *he* been then? The man who attacked her? Why hadn't Leigh seen him?

Thirteen years, she thought. Ruth had been dead for thirteen years. It seemed a lifetime. She had already missed thirteen years of living, and seeing her children grow up. She should have had those years and many more.

Why do I keep thinking of Ruth? she wondered, when it almost happened to me?

And still could. The man had not yet been caught.

But Owen would tell the police. Tomorrow they would come and ask her about it, and they would watch for him. If he were lurking, they would catch him.

Tomorrow.

She jerked awake. She had been drifting into sleep, but tomorrow was still hours away.

She listened to the now familiar sounds outside her room. The voices at the nurses' station. She knew that each station was situated at a corner with a view down every hallway. They could see the light flash above her door when she wanted them. She pulled the call button close to her left hand.

A shuffling sound as a patient walked stiffly down the hall. The ring of a bedside telephone. Voices and more voices passing her doorway. Owen had left the door half closed. She could not see into the hall, but she could hear it, alive and active.

He wouldn't dare, she thought, come again.

The conversation with Owen had worn her out. It was the first time she had talked in nearly a week. And she had had to go on talking long after she was tired.

Again she closed her eyes and almost slept. Again she woke quickly. Her body wanted to sleep, but her mind would not let it. Or perhaps it was the other way around. She listened, wondering what had waked her. Was it only fear, or had she heard something? The hospital was not fully settled down for the night. The visitors had gone, but anyone could pass unnoticed at any time, wearing white clothes. Probably stolen from the laundry. She resolved to stay awake all night, but could not stop herself . . .

She woke, fighting death. She could not breathe. Dark. Something pressed against her face. She fought, clawing and kicking. She screamed into muffled blackness. Her scream was lost. Her head swam. Her lungs pulled but could not get air. *I'm dead.*

Suddenly the pillow lightened. She gasped, a long, audible breath. Another. She stared into black eyes, winged brows.

He spoke over his shoulder. "I heard a noise. The pillow must have fallen on her face while she was sleeping."

Then he vanished and a nurse bent over her, adjusting the pillows, raising her head so she could breathe better.

"It's all right now, dear. I'll bet that gave you a scare."

She wheezed again. "He—tried—"

"Yes, it's over now. Lucky thing he heard you."

"He tried—Same—man—"

"You probably had a bad dream."

"*Listen* to me."

"I'm listening." The nurse stood back, giving her full attention.

"He tried—to kill me."

She had not made herself clear. She wanted the nurse to know about the other time, too. She lifted her bandaged hand. "He tried—to kill me."

"He tried to kill you? Are you serious?"

"Please."

"He said the pillow fell on your face. Maybe you only thought—"

"Please. He beat me. Tried to kill me. Same man."

"Oh, lord." The nurse hurried away.

Lyn drew a long breath. And another. Another. She could

not stop herself from breathing hard, trying to make up for the air she had lost.

The nurse came back with a large, block-shaped woman, probably the supervisor.

"Now what's all this?" the supervisor asked. "You're saying that someone deliberately put the pillow over your face?"

"He was pushing on it," Lyn explained weakly.

"And he beat you?"

She held up her hand. With her left hand, she indicated her still wired jaw.

"Why didn't you tell us about this before? That this was a beating?"

"Couldn't talk. Told my husband—tonight. He was going to —call police."

"There haven't been any police here asking about it."

"Maybe—tomorrow."

The kindly eyes watched her steadily. "Are you sure this is true?"

"It's *true*." Her voice ended hoarsely, in a wail.

The supervisor left. The nurse remained, again adjusting the pillows, making her comfortable.

A few minutes later, the supervisor returned.

"I've just called the police to check. There haven't been any reports."

"He *said*—"

"Now wait a minute. You told your husband and he said he was going to call the police? Let me talk to your husband. Where is he, at home?"

Lyn gave her the telephone number. Again the nurse stayed with her. This time it was a longer interval before the supervisor came back.

"Yes, he says that's what you told him." In the half darkness, the large, square face looked concerned. Probably such a thing had never happened before at Great Harbor General. "He says he didn't think there was great immediacy, since it happened several days ago, and he wanted to wait for the day shift."

"Why?" Lyn asked.

"I don't know why. I suppose he has his reasons. Now you get some sleep. We'll be watching your door for the rest of the night."

She refused medication. They would watch when they had a chance, but she knew how busy they were. She would have to watch for herself.

She felt cold after they left, as though someone had filled her with ice.

He hadn't told them. He was waiting for the day shift. She supposed it could be true. He might think that way. They would have more men on the day shift, and there would be a lot of activity, coming to the hospital, interviewing people. It might be better to wait.

But "no great immediacy," he had said. No great immediacy.

And in the meantime, the man had struck again.

=18=

The next day was Saturday. Owen came to visit her in the late morning, just after she had finished her liquid lunch.

"The children?" she asked.

"They're okay. I have a very nice woman looking after them. A college girl."

"Want to see them."

"You will as soon as you get home. I can't bring them here, they're too young."

"Neal—Is Neal doing his homework? His math?"

"I guess so. But you know, I haven't even been there in the evenings. I've been coming to see you."

"He watches television. He'll tell you he can work during television. The teacher says he doesn't finish some assignments."

"I'll remind him. How are you feeling?"

"You didn't tell the police. Man came—last night. He—"

"Yes. One of the nurses called and told me. I'm really surprised a guy like that would show his face here."

He did not believe her.

"He tried—with a pillow. He tried to kill me."

"Honey," Owen said gently, "if that guy were really trying to kill you, he'd have done it by now."

She hadn't the strength to describe what had happened. That the nurse had come in and interrupted him. She only repeated, "You didn't tell police."

"I went there this morning. I didn't think—honestly, baby, I didn't think you'd have any more trouble."

She closed her eyes to hold back tears, but could not stop them. He took her hand and patted it clumsily.

What a mess I must be, she thought. Crying, with a wired jaw.

"Anyhow," he said, "I went this morning. I wanted to give them a full report in person. They said they'd send someone over to talk to you. I'll be right here when he comes."

True to his word, Owen remained during the police interview. She could tell them no more than she had told him, except about the attack last night. They expressed surprise that Owen had not come to them sooner.

"I'm kicking myself from here to eternity," Owen said. "When I think—" He shook his head in horror. "But I never realized the guy would still be after her. It doesn't make sense."

"Evidently it makes sense to him," one of the policemen replied, clearly disapproving of people who drew their own conclusions. "We don't know what his motives are."

"How can it be anything but some punk trying to get in the house? She doesn't know any rough characters. She was never mixed up with anybody. Hey, honey. That guy you were married to once."

"No," she said. "It's not him."

"He could have sent somebody. Maybe he has a grudge or something?"

"Not Joe. And not after all this time."

"Can you be sure?"

A grudge, she thought. Tina . . .

But she couldn't say it. Even if she could tell the policemen alone, they would ask Owen about it. Ask him what he thought, and Owen would be outraged.

It couldn't be Tina. She denied it to herself, even knowing it was probably dangerous to do so.

"What's going to happen?" Owen asked. "Are you going to put a guard on her room?"

"I doubt if we have the manpower for that," he was told. "We'll be watching for this guy. We've got a description, and we'll talk to the nurse who saw him. To protect your wife, I'd suggest you move her into a room with other people."

Owen frowned. "I don't know, she's pretty sick."

"Yes, please?" said Lyn.

"Would it make you feel better, honey?"

"Much better."

Later that day she was transferred to a room with four beds, two of which were already occupied. She hoped both the occupants were insomniacs, and would have a stream of visitors day and night.

Owen seemed constrained by the lack of privacy. He glared at the other patients and their visitors.

"It's not going to last forever," Lyn promised him. "I'll be going home in another week or so. I have to practice walking up and down the hall. Can we do that now?"

The hall was scarcely less private than the room, but he seemed grateful for the diversion. They walked to the solarium, sat for a while on a vinyl sofa and watched the other patients and their guests converse in low tones or page through dogeared magazines. Afterward they paced the corridor three more times.

The walking was repeated every night when he came to visit. She grew stronger, but still did not know how she would manage at home by herself.

"Maybe we should get a housekeeper for a while," she suggested.

"We can see how it goes," he said. "The kids and I'll pitch in, and I can ask Nancy to look in on you during the day."

"Who's Nancy?"

"She's the girl who's been taking care of the kids. She's staying with the Elliotts."

"I didn't know anybody was staying with the Elliotts."

"Just since February. A niece, or something. Marvelous girl."

She wondered how Owen had gotten to know her. She supposed she ought to be glad that Neal and Paul had a marvelous girl to look after them instead of some uncaring slob. But Owen's enthusiasm bothered her.

Still, it probably didn't mean anything. No one could have been more faithful than Owen about spending his evenings with her, helping her walk up and down the corridors and regain her strength, when undoubtedly he would rather have gone home and relaxed after a day of work and commuting.

Soon her wires were removed, and so were many of her bandages. She could walk by herself without getting dizzy. And in one more day, she was to leave for home. She did not feel physically ready to cope, but she was tired of the hospital, eager to be her own mistress in her own surroundings, and to see her children again.

Owen walked beside her now without holding her. They had strolled the length of the L-shaped corridor and were on their way back to her room, when they passed a bank of elevators.

That was where we started, she remembered. That was when he first asked me out, in an elevator, and there were three in our office building, just like this.

One of the "up" lights flashed on. A moment later, the door below it slid open. She stopped walking and clutched at Owen's arm, not knowing, at first, quite why. A laboratory cart was wheeled out from the cavernous pink interior and the doors began to close. At that moment she saw him.

"It's the man!" she cried. The young woman pushing the cart turned to look at her.

"What man?" Owen asked.

"In there! The elevator."

The elevator had gone.

"It couldn't be," he said. "What would he be doing—"

"It was! I saw his eyes. He was starting to get off and then he saw me. Why don't you do something?"

"What can I do? If he saw you, he'll be gone by now. Anyway, I don't believe it. You've gotten so scared, you're probably seeing him everywhere."

She felt her legs begin to buckle. "Maybe I am. I'm sorry. I don't know what to do."

"It's all right, darling. I know you're upset and frightened. Don't worry about it. You'll be going home tomorrow."

"I don't want to go home."

"But—"

"I'll be there alone."

"Not for the weekend. Tomorrow's Saturday. I'll be there Saturday and Sunday. And then, if you want, I'll get a housekeeper to stay with you."

"Promise?"

"I promise."

He half carried her to her room and helped her into bed. He seemed in a hurry to leave. She did not try to keep him. He would come tomorrow morning, and then she would go home with him and he would keep her safe.

=19=

Neal and Paul ran to meet her, nearly knocking her over. She found herself starting to cry. "I *missed* you," she told them, and remembered that, long ago, she had said those words to Owen.

She went to bed immediately, but the twins would not leave her alone. Neal brought his homework to finish in her room. "I won't watch television," he promised. Paul was writing a story and illustrating it with colored markers. Lyn was only vaguely aware of Nancy Lehrman, a young, smiling girl with golden brown hair, who wished her well and hoped she would be comfortable.

As if it's her house, Lyn thought indignantly after Nancy left to be driven home by Owen. And she wondered why Nancy needed driving home, if she was staying with the Elliotts, who lived only a few hundred yards away. It was true that in the suburbs no one walked—but why was Owen taking so long?

He returned more than an hour later with his arms full of groceries. He told her, as though praising a conscientious child, that Nancy had helped him shop. At least Nancy had not come back with him to help cook. The family spent a quiet weekend together, with only the twins talking occasionally of Nancy. On Monday a large, efficient woman named Mrs. Sylvester came to take over the housework and keep Lyn company.

Lyn insisted upon having the outside doors locked at all times, to the inconvenience of everyone else. At home in her

own surroundings, where she was not accustomed to lying in
bed, she quickly grew stronger and would soon be able to
manage for herself. She concealed this growing self-sufficiency
from Owen, for she wanted Mrs. Sylvester to stay. The housekeeper was a day worker and Owen rarely saw her. He only
paid her salary and complained good-naturedly about the ex-
pense.

Lyn had been home for several days when Leigh Elliott
came to visit.

Leigh was an expansive woman in her fifties, with a husky
voice, casually graying hair, and a penchant for bright plaid
slacks.

"It's sweater weather," she crowed, flapping the corners of
her red cardigan as Lyn opened the door. "I just love spring. It
makes everything worthwhile, even winter. You ought to get
out more, you silly girl, what are you doing inside on a day like
this?"

"Didn't Owen tell you?" Lyn conducted her guest to the living room where Mrs. Sylvester, without being asked, served
them coffee.

"Tell me what? Look, honey, I'm really sorry I never got to
visit you in the hospital, but I just can't stand hospitals, know
what I mean? They depress me." She paused to study Lyn's
face. "Boy, you really took a beating. What did you do, hit the
windshield?"

"That's what I mean. Didn't Owen tell you?"

"I've hardly seen Owen, except when he thanked me for
calling the police, but good grief, what did he expect me to do,
leave you there?"

"He didn't tell you." It jarred, and she did not know why.
Was it so extraordinary that he hadn't broadcast the gruesome
truth? But why not at least to Leigh, who had practically been
on the scene?

"It *was* a beating," she said. "That's exactly what it was. A
man waiting in the garage—"

Leigh's mouth fell open. She reached out to clutch Lyn's wrist. "You're *kidding!*"

"No, I'm not. And I don't know why Owen didn't say anything." Lyn related the details of the attack. She told about seeing the man again in the hospital, about the pillow on her face.

"That's why I want Mrs. Sylvester. I don't really need her all that badly, but—"

"My *dear*," Leigh exclaimed sympathetically. "You're so brave. If it was me, I'd lock myself in the bathroom and never come out. Why don't you go away for a while? Go on a cruise."

"I want to be here with the twins, and I can't take them out of school. But I just don't—Owen thought someone might have a grudge against me. But I wonder if it might be someone with a grudge against Owen."

"Oh, *yes*. Because of the first wife."

"I don't know. That was thirteen years ago."

"I see what you mean. It'd have to be a psychopath. Well, some people are. I hope they catch him real quick. Listen, you're not afraid to go out with Owen, are you?"

"Not as long as he's with me. Why?"

"So you'll be coming to our party."

"What party?"

Leigh's eyebrows shot up. "What's with Owen, anyway? Maybe he thought you wouldn't be up to it, but I'm surprised he didn't at least ask. Saturday we're having some people in. Just a little get-together to meet Nancy."

"I've met Nancy."

Again the eyebrows. Lyn had spoken more curtly than she meant to. She could not forget that Nancy had been in her home while she had not. But that was only to care for the children. Still, she wondered why Owen could not have hired someone like Mrs. Sylvester to begin with.

"I just mean—I'd love it. She seems like a very sweet girl, and she was nice to look after the twins. What time Saturday?"

Owen was dismayed that evening when she mentioned the party.

"But, darling, you're not ready. You shouldn't be running around like that. And your face—"

The bruises on her face were still visible, faint splotches of reddish brown, the color of stewed plums.

"I can wear makeup," she said. "And it's mostly going to be my friends, the people from around here. They won't mind if I look awful. Don't you want to go?"

"Well, of course." He tried to meet her eyes and was unable to. From that, she knew he had planned to go without her.

And what had he meant to do, leave her at home alone, with the twins asleep, for the killer to strike again?

The twins . . . It frightened her. If someone had a grudge against Owen—

But so far, no one had made any attempt against Owen's children. It was Owen's wives they were after.

His attitude made her all the more determined. By Saturday, he had resigned himself to the fact of her going to the party.

They engaged Mrs. Sylvester to stay with the twins. Lyn covered her face carefully with a heavy foundation cream, but could not hide all the bruises. She wore an ankle-length skirt of dark green velvet, a soft white blouse, and the emerald pendant Owen had given her for Christmas long ago.

She remembered the girl she had been then, trusting, naive, and barely out of the nest. He had seemed beyond her reach. Now he had been her husband for twelve years.

And Ruth had been dead for thirteen. Ruth, who should have lived . . .

She *must* stop thinking about it. She had been dwelling on Ruth too much, after the attack upon herself.

"Keep the doors locked," she admonished Mrs. Sylvester as they left.

Owen insisted upon taking the car, although they could easily have walked. He was being very careful of her. "I might have lost you," he pointed out.

The Elliotts' living room was already crowded when they arrived. Leigh must have told everyone on Purdue Lane about the attack. They clustered around Lyn, exclaiming, asking her how she was, and wondering why Owen had kept it a secret.

"He didn't know," she defended him. "I couldn't talk for almost a week, and on top of that, I didn't remember it for a while. You know, when you get hit on the head—" She turned to Owen as though to show him: See? They don't mind my bruises. I'm a sensation.

But Owen's attention was on the far side of the room. She saw a head of bright hair, one bare shoulder. Nancy had her back to them. She wore a white dress with only one sleeve.

"Eye-catching style," murmured Lyn.

"Mm?" said Owen, bemused. Pretending not to have noticed. "Can I get you anything?"

"No, thanks. I'll help myself." Leigh's parties were always catered. A maid was passing out canapés, while a circulating bartender took orders for drinks.

"Would you like to sit down?" Owen asked.

"No, I don't think so. I want to see everybody first."

He stood beside her, catching her elbow when someone wanted to pass, ready to prop her up if she should start to collapse.

"I told her she ought to stay home," he explained to the couple from across the road. "It's a long haul, getting back on your feet after a thing like that."

"I feel fine," she insisted again and again.

Leigh Elliott's voice boomed out, "*Hi,* there, how's it going? I love that color." Nodding at the dark green skirt. "Did you meet my niece? She and Owen already know each other."

Nancy, beside her, smiling and delicately perfumed.

"My niece, Nancy Lehrman," Leigh introduced her. "This is Lyn Holdridge, Owen's wife."

"Hi," said Lyn. "Yes, we met when I came home from the hospital. I told you that, Leigh."

"Well, I didn't know what sort of condition you were in at the time," Leigh apologized.

"Anyway, it's nice to see you, Nancy. And thanks for looking after my kids."

Leigh drifted away and Nancy remained. The smile was replaced by a look of concern.

"How are you feeling, Mrs. Holdridge? Owen said he didn't think you'd be coming tonight."

Owen? This child was probably younger than Tina, and calling him by his first name. And Owen undoubtedly encouraged it. He liked to see himself as a fountain of youth.

"I feel all right," said Lyn. "I don't know why Owen thought I wouldn't come. He didn't even bother asking me. I had to get a special invitation from your aunt."

"I think he was worried because you have that woman coming in every day. He thought if you really felt like yourself—"

"I have that woman coming in every day," Lyn replied sharply, "for my own security. Maybe he didn't take the trouble to mention what put me in the hospital to begin with."

Nancy gave a stricken gasp. "Oh, yes. Oh, that was terrible. It's got everybody nervous, all up and down the road."

That piece of news provided Lyn with a certain amount of satisfaction. It was reassuring, too, to think that the attacker might have been a burglar preying on a well-to-do neighborhood, and the victim could have been anyone, not just herself.

But her reassurance was short-lived. Why, then, had he followed her to the hospital?

Nancy continued to hover. "You're looking better than when I first saw you, but you still have those bruises on your face. That must have been awful."

"It was." Lyn thought perhaps it was time to change the subject, and rallied herself.

"How long have you been living here with Leigh and Wally?"

"Since February. I'm taking some classes at Hofstra."

"Where are you from?"

"Indiana. But I don't think I'll go back there. I've gotten hooked on the East. I'd love to get a job and an apartment in New York."

"Lots of luck."

She meant it. She felt uneasy, and was not sure why. Perhaps because Owen seemed so well acquainted with this girl, who had been living here since February.

Which was not so long ago, she reminded herself. It was April now, and she had been in the hospital for more than half of March.

"You're seeing New York at the worst time," she said. "And you still like it?"

"Oh, yes. It doesn't seem so bad to me." Nancy looked past her. The perfunctory smile turned to a genuine glow.

Owen came up beside them. His eyes were on Nancy, answering her silently as he said to Lyn, "Are you feeling all right? Don't you want to sit down?"

"I'm okay."

"I see you two are getting acquainted."

Lyn said, "That's what this party's all about, isn't it? But it must be kind of dull for you," she added to Nancy. "There's hardly anybody here your age. I guess it was the best Leigh could manage in a neighborhood like this. All the young people move to the city."

"Oh, I'm enjoying it." Smiling broadly now, Nancy flashed a glance at Owen. "I think this is a wonderful bunch. And I meet plenty of, quote, young people at school."

Owen said to her, "You were talking about a job for the summer. There's a guy over there who owns a firm that makes advertising displays. Come on, I'll introduce you." He turned to Lyn. "Excuse us for a minute?"

She stood clutching her drink as the two walked away. People moved past her, sometimes obstructing her view, but still she watched. Nancy's wide-eyed fascination seemed to charm everyone. Mostly it was directed at Owen.

Lyn moved closer to the wall. She felt better, somehow, standing near a wall. As though one side of her were protected.

In an almost unnoticeable movement, Owen placed his hand possessively on Nancy's waist.

Lyn set her half-empty glass on the nearest table, pushed her way among chattering islands of people, to the dining room, where maids were setting up a buffet supper. There, French doors opened onto a terrace. She slipped outside, closed the door behind her, and walked to the end of the terrace, where it was dark. She lit a cigarette and stood watching the moonlight on the lily pond below her.

She could still hear the party, but distance and darkness kept it away from her. Where she stood, it was cool and peaceful. Too cool, in fact. She really needed her jacket, but did not want to go back inside.

The sound of a window opening made her realize that the others were not so far away, and someone else might decide to come out here. She walked down the steps that led from the terrace, and sat on the lowest one. Now they could not see her unless they stood above her, and she would hear them coming.

She stared at the pond, and wondered how Ruth had found out. It must have been all those late nights. Or the age-old lipstick on a shirt collar. Perhaps he had not been careful. Perhaps he had wanted her to know. Had he really asked for a divorce? He had not asked Lyn. Maybe it hadn't yet reached that stage.

She ached at the thought of her children at home. Why must this happen to them?

At least Ruth had not had to see them together, but she had known, nevertheless. Lyn remembered her coming into the office that day.

"The children need him. He's their father and they need him."

It was because of them that Ruth had refused to give up Owen. Probably she figured he would get over it in time.

And it appeared that he had—thirteen years later. He was over his infatuation with Lyn and on to someone else.

She threw her cigarette into the lily pond and it sizzled out. Leigh would have her head for throwing cigarettes into the lily pond.

Leigh's niece . . . But Leigh couldn't know anything about this. She was a friend. Lyn's friend as well as Owen's.

Anyhow, Lyn thought bitterly, who would condone her niece getting involved with a married man old enough to be her father? It was disgusting. They'd never allow it, if they knew.

With an angry toss she disposed of the next cigarette, which she had barely smoked.

She could take the children and leave. She could go back to her mother, who lived alone and widowed in that house in Elmhurst. There would be plenty of room. The boys could go to school there. It would be different, but . . .

Why should I? If he doesn't want me anymore, let him be the one to move out.

She felt tears coming. She must not cry out here, it would streak her makeup. She put her hand to her face and remembered the bruises. Her jaw was still tender. She lit another cigarette and huddled, shivering, on the step. She was freezing, probably catching pneumonia, but she did not want to go in until she had composed herself.

Something moved in the bushes beyond the garden. She stiffened, paralyzed. Looking down, she saw the cigarette glowing in her hand. She flicked it into the pond.

Slowly she stood up, ready to run. The thing moved again. She clutched at the wall beside her. Something crashed through the underbrush, away from her.

An animal, thank God, only an animal. A rabbit or raccoon. Her heart pounded and her teeth chattered with cold. She blotted away her tears, lit another cigarette, and went into the house.

They were lining up at the buffet table. Leigh hailed her. "Grab a plate, hon. Do you need any help?"

"No, thanks. I'll be okay." How many times had she said it this evening? Probably she would never be okay again.

Just off the entryway was a small powder room. She closed herself inside and checked her face. The bruises seemed to have become darker, or perhaps her makeup was rubbing off. She had no remedy with her except pressed powder, and it didn't cover very well. She wished she had not come to the party.

The doorknob turned. Someone else wanted the bathroom. She would have liked to stay hidden all night. She checked her face once more and left, forcing a bright smile.

Owen was in the dining room. She looked about for Nancy, but did not see her.

"You okay?" Owen asked. She would scream if she heard that once more. "Tell me if you want to go home."

"Later." It would not be fair to drag him away before he had eaten. Whatever might be happening, she still loved him. But she added, "I'd like to talk to you." That would give him something to think about.

They joined the line at the table and were faced with an array of hot dishes and salads. She took a spoonful of rice and topped it with chicken curry.

"That's all?" asked Owen.

"I can go back later." She gritted her teeth. She had had enough of being treated like an invalid. They returned to the living room where they could sit down, and ate together, although they seemed to have little to say to each other.

Almost an hour later, when they had finished their coffee, she announced her readiness to leave.

"But," she added, "I want you to stay home with me. If you're coming back here, then Mrs. Sylvester has to stay."

"Poor darling." It was almost a reflex by now, that "poor darling." But her concern was not for herself alone. There were the children. And even Owen could scarcely want to lose a second wife so brutally.

Nevertheless—

Ruth's death had been very convenient for his plans at the time.

But not that way, she protested. *He couldn't have wanted it that way.*

Polite good-byes to Leigh, to Wally, and Nancy, and all the others. Then they were in the car, and the night was cold. She wondered how she had managed to sit on those steps for as long as she had.

"When did you meet Nancy?" she asked.

"Nancy? Oh, I don't know."

"She's been here since February."

"I know. I think I met her coming out on the train with Wally. He introduced us."

"Is Hofstra in the city?"

"It's in Hempstead. Why? What's this big deal about Nancy?"

She did not reply. There was no need. He would know what she was talking about, whatever he pretended.

"How old is she?"

"Who?" Their car glided up the driveway, past the curve with the steep drop on one side, where she had almost died. Twice. But the first time had been her own fault.

"Twenty-one," he said.

"Twenty-*one?*"

"What's wrong with that?"

"She's much younger than Tina."

"Is she?" He asked it mildly, almost as though he had not been listening.

"You seem very attracted to her. And she was just crazy about you, I noticed."

"Is that how it looked to you?"

"Yes, it did. And don't tell me I'm wrong. My memory isn't that short. You like younger women, don't you?"

The garage door slid open under the bidding of his remote control, and he drove the car inside. He turned off the engine and patted her leg.

"Aren't you a younger woman?" he asked teasingly.

"That's what I mean. I was. Now I'm over thirty." She caught his hand as he reached to open the door. "I want to talk about this, Owen."

"Won't your Mrs. Sylvester wonder why we're stuck in the garage?"

"Let her wonder," Lyn said angrily. "She can come out and look, if she wants to. We've got to get this settled, and I don't want the twins to hear."

He turned toward her, resting his arm on the back of the seat. "My dear girl—"

"I'm not a girl any more. And I think that's a big part of the problem."

"You're *my* girl, aren't you?"

"Are you in love with Nancy?"

"Now what gave you—"

"Look, will you stop evading? I'll bet you evaded with Ruth, too. I really mean this, I have to know. It's my whole life we're talking about."

"Your life? What do you mean by that?"

The phrase had strange echoes. That had been her reason for marrying Joe—because she wanted a real life.

"What I mean is, I'm not going to—" It was all echoing crazily. A full circle in the fourteen years she had known him.

"I'm not going to share you. I don't want the leftovers. I don't want you to be married to me and in love with someone else."

"So what does that mean?"

He knew damn well what it meant.

"I just want to know," she said. "Truthfully. I want to know where I stand."

"Aren't you making rather a scene over a harmless bit of attention? After all, she was the guest of honor."

"It's not harmless." She groped in her purse for a handkerchief. "Because you see, Owen, I know you. Remember? I was there once, too. And I want to know right off whether I should—"

"You should—?"

"Start thinking about a divorce."

He threw back his head and laughed. "Now that's ridiculous, isn't it?"

"You tell me."

"I'm telling you it's ridiculous. Come on into the house, you're starting to shiver."

=20

On Sunday she drove her car for the first time since the accident. She took the twins to a soccer game and stayed to watch them play. She had been disappointed that Owen had not wanted to go. It might have brought them closer again. Perhaps he wanted to spend the time with Nancy. It must have been fun for him, with his wife in the hospital and Nancy looking after the children.

When she drove home, alone because the twins were celebrating their victory with friends, she half expected to find Nancy there, maybe guiltily straightening her hair and tucking in her shirt.

Instead she heard his voice on the telephone.

"No, don't hurt her," he was saying. "I don't want you to hurt her."

She froze, her hand on the door. He was in the dining room and she had come through the back entryway. She closed the door noiselessly and tiptoed across the floor. A board creaked under the vinyl tiles.

"Just a minute." He came into view, holding the telephone receiver on its long, curled cord.

"Oh, hi. I didn't know you were back."

She stared at him, unable to speak.

"Where are the kids?" he asked.

"They went to Burger King."

To the unseen person at the other end of the wire, he said, "Look, my wife just got home. I'll talk to you later."

"That's all right," she told him quickly. "Finish your call. You don't have to do anything about me."

"It's finished." He hung up the phone and came into the kitchen. His body, in jeans, was still slender and firm. She had wondered what a twenty-one-year-old girl could see in him, but he had lost none of his physical appeal. Added to it was a mature charm, a youthful vivacity, and the courtly manners that so many younger men lacked.

"Was it Nancy?" she asked.

He snorted with impatience. "Will you get Nancy off your mind?"

"Then I don't know why you had to stop talking as soon as I came home."

Don't hurt her. I don't want you to hurt her.

It could have been anything. Tina's husband, perhaps. She had no way of knowing who he meant by "her."

His face looked bleak. "I wanted to see if you were all right. It's your first time out."

She had no answer, although she still doubted. Perhaps the bleak look was because of her accusations.

"I'm fine," she said, echoing the night before, and started toward the bedroom.

"Good." He followed her. "How was the game?"

"We won."

"Glad to hear it." He stopped and let her go on. She wondered if he would go back to the phone. But of course not, now. He would be afraid she might listen on the extension.

She lay down on the bed, her arm over her forehead. She wondered what was wrong with her. Everything seemed so normal—and yet not normal. It had not been normal since Ruth was killed. She knew that now. Murder was not an accident, and it had happened in this house. It had happened to the woman who held her position before her. Beyond that, she did not want to think.

She had not saved any of the news stories about the murder and the trial. It was a period in her life and Owen's that she preferred to forget. She ought to have known it was not so easily erased.

On Monday she left Mrs. Sylvester in charge of the house and drove to the Great Harbor Public Library.

They knew who she was, of course. Her picture had been in the papers during the trial, and they were aware of her marriage to Owen. As a young bride she had not bothered with the library, but when her children were old enough for picture books she had taken out a card and made regular visits with them.

The librarian, a plump woman named Mrs. Molsap, looked at her curiously when she asked about the newspapers of thirteen years ago.

"We have those back dates on microfilm," Mrs. Molsap said. "We have the *Times*, but I think for that we also have the *Post* and *Daily News* because it happened right here in Great Harbor."

Lyn waited while the appropriate containers were unearthed, and then she was seated at the library's only microfilm-reading machine.

"That was a terrible thing," Mrs. Molsap volunteered as she threaded the film. "Of course you didn't know Mrs. Holdridge. *That* Mrs. Holdridge."

"I met her once," said Lyn. "She was sweet."

"A terrible thing."

Questions hung unasked and unanswered as Mrs. Molsap demonstrated how to use the machine. Undoubtedly she would have liked to know the reason for Lyn's sudden interest. Perhaps she had heard about the attack. And there was no mistaking the bruises on Lyn's face.

Lyn spun the film through the reel until she came to the date of Ruth's murder. Then she slowed and wound it carefully to the next day. The newspaper report. *Long Island Housewife Found Slain.*

It was strange to see it all again. She had almost memorized the words at the time. For days the reports ran on. The police investigation. The unearthing of the affair with a secretary, Mrs. Lynette Singleton. It was as though she were reading about someone else.

Poor Joe Singleton. Not only the police, but the reporters had interviewed him, adding humiliation to hurt. God, I'm sorry, Joe.

She wondered where he was now, what he was doing. She hoped he was happy, whatever it was.

After that, interest died down until the trial. She removed the reel from the machine and inserted another.

The wrangling of the lawyers, the request for a change of venue, which was denied. The selection of the jury. She read through it quickly, while a lump of dread grew in her throat.

And then the trial itself. Here, too, almost every word was familiar.

But different, too. She did not remember this at all—the insurance. Had she forgotten? Or simply blotted it out at the time? Half a million dollars of insurance. On Ruth's life.

He said it was because of the children. That was what he testified and told reporters.

The dates. She had to read it several times before she saw it. Almost a year before the death. How could anyone be suspicious of that? A whole year.

But it was just after Lyn went to work in his office. That was the first policy. And two more soon afterward.

The prosecution had leaned on it. She was beginning to remember now. They had made a big issue of that insurance.

But the defense had made it sound so reasonable. Two young children. His wife's worth as a homemaker. After her death he had had to hire someone to look after the children.

For a year. Until he married Lyn.

Five hundred thousand dollars. How many years of housekeeping would it buy? The children were half-grown by the time he acquired those policies.

The lump in her throat was pulsating now. She remembered last fall. Was it November? He had thought they ought to have more insurance on themselves. For the children's sake. He said he would take out another policy on his own life, and one on hers.

That was the only time he mentioned it. She did not know whether he had actually done it. Again he made it sound reasonable—a life insurance policy that converted to an endowment at age sixty-five.

She read through the rest of the trial stories. She read her own testimony. She had laid herself bare before the public, and that, she thought, had saved him.

The prosecution had gone down flailing, suggesting that he planned it that way.

Of course he hadn't. He wanted to protect her honor. He cared about her.

But why the elaborate arrangements that morning? She remembered wondering at the time. She could have taken the papers in to work with her. Owen could have signed them and Mr. Tannen notarized them, and then she could have delivered them herself to the office on Nineteenth Street.

Perhaps he had wanted to see her. And it had been fun, having him come in the morning, and then driving into town with him.

But why that of all mornings?

He *couldn't* have known. It had simply happened when it did. He couldn't have known it would happen at all.

She remembered, later in the office, that he kept looking at his watch.

Expecting a call. Expecting the housekeeper . . .

Everything had been strange that day. The housekeeper had been sick. It was Tina who found the body.

Looking at his watch. *Because he had a lunch date.* He would not have had to go through that elaborate procedure to create an alibi. He would have been in the office in any case. It had only hurt him by making the day stand out.

But it had helped, too, by making it look as though he was hiding something, and then her testimony showed what he was hiding. A mere sexual encounter. An excellent smokescreen if he was really hiding a murder.

Had he planned that, too?

No, she thought. *He loves me.* And he had been fond of Ruth. It was crazy of her to think those things.

But the insurance. She would have to find out about the insurance.

She returned the microfilm to its box, thanked Mrs. Molsap, and left the library. The sun hurt her eyes as she stood outside, wondering what to do next.

= 21 =

Mrs. Sylvester left a ham casserole baking in the oven when she went home that evening. A salad, already mixed, was in the refrigerator.

"This is a lot of luxury," Owen remarked as Lyn set the casserole on the dinner table. "It's nice for you, baby, but I don't know if we're really in that league. How long are we planning to keep her?"

"She'll have to leave in about a month," Lyn replied. "Her daughter's having a baby." She had not meant to tell him when Mrs. Sylvester was leaving.

"Why does she have to leave?" asked Neal, watching dubiously as his mother served the casserole. "I like her."

"I don't want any of that," Paul announced.

"I like her, too," said Lyn. "But her daughter's having a baby and Mrs. Sylvester promised to look after the other children."

"I said I don't want any of that."

"You eat three bites, and then if you don't like it you don't have to finish it."

"A whole month?" Owen's fingers moved rapidly as he multiplied the weeks by Mrs. Sylvester's salary, which he considered generous. "You seem to be managing very well already," he added mildly.

"I can get around," she replied, "but my hand still doesn't work right, and you know I don't want to be here by myself."

She watched his face to see how he would react. He frowned thoughtfully and helped himself to the salad.

"Can hardly blame you," he said, "but I don't see how we can keep this up forever."

"Just until the man is caught?"

"What man?" Neal asked. "The man who beat you up?"

"I think he's dropped out of sight. Probably left town." Owen smiled at her across the table. It was a warm smile, meant to encourage her.

"But he's still running around loose. And he did come at me in the hospital."

"He did?" Paul exclaimed. The twins hadn't known about that.

"Or you thought he did," said Owen.

"Listen, I recognized his face."

"With a mask on. You told me his face was half covered. And he didn't really do anything. So maybe, when you were already—"

"Yes, he did. The pillow."

"What pillow?" asked Paul.

"You might have imagined it," Owen suggested. "You told me you were asleep, and you only woke up to find him taking the pillow off you."

"I—"

Not in front of the children. They were already staring at her, alarmed.

"Eat your dinner," she told them.

"Yes, guys," Owen added. "It's funny, when we want you to hear what we're saying, you don't."

We shouldn't have been talking about it, she thought, worrying what their immature minds might make of the whole thing. One attack on their mother was enough.

She watched Owen playing games with them, trying to get them to eat. She had been so full of fears, suspecting everybody, even him.

He loves me, she reminded herself. *We went through so much together.*

He had only been kind to Nancy, in his own way, because she had looked after the children. Some men were like that, more demonstrative than others. It didn't mean anything.

But there was the insurance . . .

"You know," she said as the children performed their assigned chore of clearing the table, "people in hospitals don't wear surgical masks just anywhere. They only wear them in the operating rooms."

Owen sat back in his chair and lit a cigarette. "Maybe he had a cold and didn't want to expose the patients."

"You think of everything, don't you? Why did he run away the first time, when the nurse came in? Why did he come back?"

"Have you seen him since you got out?"

"No. I don't think so."

"Then it was probably just a hospital employee, and you were overwrought."

That could be. But she had known those eyes.

And now? The police were looking for him. Of course he would stay out of sight. Waiting for a chance.

She watched Owen calmly smoking, and remembered another time when he had argued. It was long ago. About Tina, distraught over her mother's death. Any parent would have wanted to help his child. But Owen had refused. No psychologist for Tina. He had let her suffer.

Afraid, perhaps, of what might be revealed.

Paul came in, carrying the dessert plates. Neal followed with a pineapple upside down cake. The two little faces, so exactly alike. So like her own. Would they be left motherless, too?

Owen asked, "What are you thinking about?"

She shuddered.

He stubbed out his cigarette. "Is it that bad?"

"I—guess so."

"Well, by all means," he said, "we'll find somebody else when Sylvester leaves."

She studied him as she passed him his plate. Did he really mean it? Would he be willing to keep a companion with her indefinitely?

"Thank you. But it wouldn't have to be forever. Only until they catch him."

She did not know what made her say that. They might never catch him. Or there might be another.

Another burglar. It could happen any time. Or a car might jump the curb. You never knew when you were going to get it. But the fact remained, you couldn't spend your life in a state of panic.

She felt easier after that.

Until later, as she was loading the dishwasher, and again remembered the insurance.

A half million dollars on Ruth's life. It was not unreasonable to take out insurance on the life of a homemaker-mother, but it was odd that there had been so much, and that Ruth had died soon afterward. She wondered that she had not paid more attention at the time.

She thought about it during the night as he slept beside her, breathing heavily. Alternately she loved him and feared him. She did not know, and she had to know.

In the morning she waited until he had left to catch his train. The children were on their way to school. She told Mrs. Sylvester that she would be gone for the better part of the day. Then she drove herself to the station and caught a train for New York City, several trains later than Owen's.

She emerged from Pennsylvania Station into the traffic and crowds of Manhattan. She had not been in town for months. It carried her back to those years when she worked there, a young girl in love with an older, married man.

And then she thought: Is that Nancy? Does she really love him? Does she think I'm in the way, and do they talk about the time when he can get it "straightened out"? Does he tell her

I'm frigid, and nothing but a mother, that I don't care about him anymore?

She took a crosstown bus to Madison Avenue. Stepping off it, she felt exposed, as though Owen could see her and know what she was doing.

The man she had come to visit was an independent agent. A Mr. Stoddard. She knew that much. He might be out of the office, but she had not wanted to call first and make an appointment. She did not want anyone to know she was coming.

Stoddard. She looked for his name on the building directory. Stoddard, Wm. He was the same man she had dealt with when she worked for Owen all those years ago.

She took an elevator to the fourteenth floor and entered a carpeted reception room. The receptionist, a sleek brunette who looked more like a store mannequin than a person, asked if she might be of help.

"Mr. Stoddard. Is he in? I'd like to see him, please."

The inevitable question. "Do you have an appointment?"

"No," replied Lyn, "I only want to see him for a minute. My husband is a long-time client of Mr. Stoddard's. There's something I have to ask him."

She wished she had dressed more elegantly, instead of in a polyester pantsuit, but it didn't seem to matter. Mr. Stoddard was a salesman, courting sales with a salesman's manner. After some negotiation between the receptionist and others, she was ushered into his office to have her hand enthusiastically pumped and herself received like visiting royalty.

"It's so nice to *see* you, Lyn. How are you and how are those two little rascals?"

She could not help smiling. "They're fine. As rascally as ever. And—"

Before she could mention herself, his face changed.

"I heard you had a terrible accident. How are you feeling? That was an awful thing. Maybe Owen should put in some kind of barrier along that driveway."

So he still thought it was an accident. She would not disabuse him. She agreed about the barrier, and then asked her question.

"Owen talked a little while ago about taking out more insurance, especially on me. I was wondering if he did it."

"Yes. Yes, he did. He took out another policy on you, and one on himself. And he increased—"

"Another? How can he take out insurance on me without my knowing? Don't I have to sign something?"

"Owen and I have been doing business for a long time. He's a big believer in insurance."

"You didn't answer my question. Don't I have anything to say about whether I'm insured? Don't I have to sign it?"

"You did, honey. I have your signature right on the thing. Maybe you don't remember."

"I certainly don't." She wondered who had signed it for her. "And what were you starting to say about increasing?"

"The existing policies. He increased the amounts by quite a lot. You know, with money getting worth less all the time—"

"Didn't you think it was kind of strange?"

"Strange? Why?"

"All that insurance on me. How much is there?"

"Of course I don't think insurance is strange. It's my business. And they're all endowments at sixty-five. That's insurance for you, dear. Remember that."

He added the further reminder that Owen was a few years older than she was, so the endowment policies were a form of pension for her.

"If I live that long," she commented. He showed no reaction, although he must have known what she was driving at with her inquiry. He was the one who had testified at Owen's trial about the amount of insurance on the life of Ruth Holdridge.

She asked again, "How much is there altogether?"

"Altogether? He's paying an awful lot. There's the both of you, and the house, the two cars, but I don't handle car insurance. And you know, those endowments are more expensive than regular term life, but of course it pays off in the long run."

"I want to know how much there is on me. Just me. I don't care about the rest of it."

"Just you. Well, let's see now." He picked up the phone and gave the request to his secretary.

While they waited for the results, he asked about her accident. She did not tell him it wasn't an accident. It would not do to have him alerted to her suspicions.

She might have gotten him on her side, but she didn't think so. He was solidly behind Owen. He, too, would have insisted that it was a burglar.

"You went over that same embankment a few years ago, didn't you?" he asked.

"Yes, but it was icy then. This time—I don't know."

She was spared the need for further evasions by the entrance of the secretary, who handed him a sheet of paper. It had not taken long.

He frowned at the paper for a moment. Then he said, "Are you ready? You're a valuable woman, dear. Seven hundred fifty thousand dollars."

Three-quarters of a million. It was more than there had been on Ruth. No wonder Owen complained about the housekeeper. He needed all his money for insurance premiums.

And there was double indemnity for accidental death, she supposed.

She opened her mouth. She was going to say: *How can he expect to get away with it twice?*

She said nothing. Bill Stoddard was grinning as though he were proud of her.

"Far above rubies," he said.

"What?"

"Don't you know that? It's from the Bible. 'Who can find a virtuous woman? For her price is far above rubies.' I guess that's you, dear."

"I'm not exactly virtuous. "

But she had been virtuous with Owen, if not with Joe. She had done nothing to deserve what was happening to her.

And neither had Ruth.

"Thanks, Bill." She held out her hand for another of his vigorous shakes. "I appreciate your time and everything."

"All satisfied now? Every question answered?"

"Every question you can answer."

"Good, then. It was nice to see you. Drop in again sometime." He followed her to the reception room and stood smiling until the door closed behind her.

=22=

Owen was reading a contract when the call came in.

"Mr. Holdridge," said the high, youthful voice of his new secretary, "it's a Mr. Stoddard on two. Will you talk to him?"

"Okay." He pressed the flashing button on his telephone. "Hi, Bill. How are you doing?"

As he listened, something began to prickle the back of his neck. Lyn here in town? He hadn't thought she felt up to it. He almost asked, "Are you sure?" But of course Bill was sure. You don't make a mistake about a thing like that.

He managed a small laugh as Bill described the interview. "What'd she say? Tell me exactly what she said." He tried to sound merely amused at this ridiculous whim of his wife's.

"Well, first she wondered how you could take out insurance on her without her knowing. She says, 'Don't I have to sign something?' And then she wanted to know the total."

"What did she *say?*"

"She said, 'How much altogether?' Said it twice."

"And you told her?"

"Sure. Why not? I kidded her, said she was a real treasure."

"You told her the whole amount?"

"Look, Owen, I had to put my secretary on it. With Lyn sitting right there, I couldn't tell the girl to give me half the figure, now could I?"

"Jesus," said Owen. He felt as though he had been operated on by a steamroller. Even half the figure would sound peculiar to Lyn. She must have remembered that stuff at the trial. She must have—

"Did she say why she wanted to know?"

"Not a word," replied Bill, "and I didn't ask. Maybe it was that accident of hers. Scared her a little. If you were a wife, wouldn't you want to know what you're worth?"

If I wanted her to know, I'd tell her, dammit.

"Anyhow," Bill continued, "I just thought it might be of interest to you that she was asking."

"Yeah, right, Bill, I'm glad you told me." He tried to think of something else to say, something that would make light of the whole thing.

But leave it to Bill to fill in the gaps. "I don't know what was going on in her head, but I made sure she understood they were all endowments, you know?"

Owen knew. He wondered if Bill did, exactly. At least he knew enough to tell him about Lyn's visit. Maybe he did that for everybody who took out three-quarters of a million on his wife.

Again he tried to chuckle. It sounded forced.

"How'd she take it? Was she surprised?" God, what a stupid way to ask that question. He had to know, but he could have worded it better.

"Dumbfounded," said Bill.

"I'll bet." The chuckle came over better this time. "Didn't know she was going to be a rich widow someday, did she?"

"Widow?"

"I'm a lot older than she is, remember."

"Not so much," Bill said consolingly. "You'll both be rich. You'll have a villa in Palm Beach. Invite me down some weekend, okay?"

So at least Bill didn't think anything was amiss. Just a guy who felt better with a lot of insurance—that was how he saw Owen.

Like that other time, with Ruth. If Bill thought anything of it, he never said so. His testimony at the trial had been completely dispassionate—as it should have been. No value judgments, no conjectures or conclusions. A man of fact.

Yet he'd figured out enough to let Owen know about this visit. Owen wondered exactly what it was he had figured.

Even more immediately, what had Lyn figured?

She walked back along Thirty-fourth Street, not knowing what to do. She was heading toward Penn Station, and home, and perhaps danger, but she was not sure. He was danger, or safety. How could she know? Either he loved her or he wanted her dead.

He loved her or loved her not. That silly thing with the daisy. She had never imagined that it could be a question of life or death.

Finally she entered the station, and on impulse, went to find a telephone book.

He might not be listed. He might even be dead by now. She had no idea how old he had been that summer.

But there was his name, Brandon, T., at the address she remembered. Central Park West, so long ago.

With her throat tight, she slipped her coin into the telephone and dialed the number. Still not quite knowing what she wanted of him, she was startled when he answered.

"Mr. Brandon? This is—My name is Lynette Holdridge. I . . ."

He knew who she was. Of course he had followed the trial. Probably remembered every word of it. He might even have been there.

"I'd like to see you, Mr. Brandon. I know you probably think we have nothing to say to each other, but I'd like to see you for just a minute. Do you have time?"

He was reluctant. She expected that. But he was also, apparently, curious, for he agreed to her request. He must be a fine, brave man, she thought. It sickened her when she remembered how they had used his apartment.

She took the subway and reached his building in fifteen minutes. The doorman directed her to the floor. She had forgotten the apartment number, but remembered which door was his.

He opened it, a tall, vigorous-looking man in a white turtle-neck sweater. Despite his steel-gray hair, he did not seem old at all. She saw little resemblance between father and daughter.

He shook her hand almost automatically, as though polite-ness were a habit of his, and invited her in. She looked about, remembering. The bubbling fish tank was gone, the slipcovers changed, but otherwise the room was the same.

"How did you know where to find me?" he asked. "How did you know about me?"

She took a breath and tried to look at him, but could not.

"I was here," she said. "With Owen. You went to Florida and he was watering the plants."

She wanted to say more, to explain herself, but there was nothing to explain. He was silent for a moment, and then, still distantly polite, asked her to sit down.

She took a chair, and he seated himself on the couch.

"I know it's terrible of me to bother you," she began. He nodded a disclaimer.

"I just don't know what to do." She found the words coming more quickly. "A little while ago I was in the hospital. A man beat me up, then put me in my car and tried to wreck the car. It didn't work, but I was in the hospital for about three weeks, and I saw the same man. I think he was still after me. One time I woke up and he was holding a pillow over my face. He told the nurse the pillow fell on me and he was taking it off, and she believed him, but I know it was the same man. Owen insists it was a burglar. He thinks there's no more danger, but I—I'm afraid. I heard him on the phone telling someone, 'No, don't hurt her, I don't want you to hurt her.' I don't know if it had anything to do with me, but—"

"You're worried about Owen?"

"Yes, about Owen. Maybe I'm wrong, I don't know. But the insurance. He had a lot of insurance on Ruth, and now he has a lot on me. I just found out today."

"And?" He was still polite, clearly asking what she expected of him.

"All I want—I just want—I didn't know what to do, or who I could talk to. I just wanted to know—Do you think he—Do you think he was guilty that time?"

The dark eyes blinked and then withdrew, seeming to consider. Finally he said, with great caution, "I believe you testified that he was with you."

"Yes, he was. I don't mean he did anything personally. Do you think he could have arranged it? He might have planned the whole thing that morning, just so I'd have to testify the way I did."

"And you want to know what I think."

"Yes. Please."

"If you want the truth, Mrs. Holdridge, I've always thought your husband was responsible for the murder of my daughter, but I had no way to prove it."

He was quiet and elegant, and his words were a kick in the stomach.

"I suppose," he went on, "it would have been possible to prove it, and that's what the prosecution should have done, but it wouldn't have brought her back. I never went on the warpath with it. And there was always the chance I might have been wrong."

"I—see."

She had asked. She had known this might be the answer, but it left her feeling hollow.

"That," he added, "is my gut feeling. Obviously it's not built on any incontrovertible evidence, but it might have been. There's nothing that goes against it. Unfortunately they based their case on the premise that he did the job himself, and when you blasted that one, the whole thing fell apart. There should have been a regrouping."

"Yes, I—Yes."

She would have fought it, at the time. She would not have

believed any of it. She might even have perjured herself to save him.

Tim Brandon thought it didn't matter, after his own daughter was dead. Nothing could bring her back. He wouldn't have cared what happened to Lyn. And why should he?

"Well," she said, half standing up, "that's what I wanted to know. I appreciate—" What did she appreciate? "Your time. And your honesty."

There was to be no discussion. He made no effort to detain her, even for a moment. Probably he found her presence distasteful.

She moved toward the door, and he followed.

"I met Ruth once," she said. "I thought she was sweet."

He nodded. "She was."

"If I thought—" No, that was getting too close. "You see, I never realized. He always said the nicest things about her. I think he was really fond of her—in his way."

Don't hurt her. I don't want you to hurt her.

Fond of me, too. In his way.

"Good-bye, Mr. Brandon. And thanks. I hope—everything works out for you."

Thirteen years too late.

Again he inclined his head. It was the closest he could come to wishing the same for her.

23

After the phone call, he sat musing at his desk, the contracts and papers forgotten.

He hadn't much time. Now that she knew about the insurance, she would start putting it all together.

Why did the damn fool have to go back to the hospital after Lyn was awake? Why couldn't he damn well have finished the job?

He might have, of course, if Leigh Elliott hadn't come barging in. Probably he'd been up there hiding at the house, waiting for them all to go away. And the police, never imagining it was anything but an accident, didn't think of looking for him.

Damn lucky they didn't.

But then, that fiasco at the hospital. How the hell could one bloody fool blow it so many times? Why the hell couldn't Russ have done the job himself? He'd been so clean the first time. Knocked her out in one blow so she didn't feel the rest. Or so he said.

But Russ had turned cowardly over the years. Didn't want to touch it. Afraid his hands might shake. And so he'd turned it over to an even softer-brained lush than himself.

Not much time. He slipped the papers into a folder and pretended to dial the phone, in case they heard any of the other call. So they wouldn't think that was what sent him running. He talked briefly, then buzzed for his secretary. A sweet kid.

Beth. Not even Elizabeth. Just Beth. A sweet kid with a nice shape.

"Yes, Mr. Holdridge?"

"I've got to go out. Something's come up. I probably won't be back for the rest of the day. Just finish the work you have, and I'll give you the dictation tomorrow."

Tomorrow. Everything would be different tomorrow. Probably he wouldn't even be coming in, but he was not supposed to know that yet.

He almost forgot to take his briefcase. That would have been a mistake. He must look as if he was going out on business.

"See you," he called jauntily to the girls.

Doris Peltzer's round eyes behind rimless glasses looked up from her books. "Good-bye, Mr. Holdridge."

In the elevator, he glanced at his watch. He knew what time it was. It just seemed a habit to check his watch in the elevator, as though even that momentary enforced idleness, designed to save time, were too long.

Another delay while he waited for the crosstown subway. He should have headed for the shuttle instead of this Flushing line. The shuttle ran more frequently in off-hours.

He changed trains at Times Square and took the Seventh Avenue express, then waited again for the local at Fourteenth Street. He got off at Sheridan Square in the Village and walked along Christopher Street to Greenwich Avenue.

Moylan's Bar. It was still there, the same as always, and probably Russ Jaeger was, too. He used the place like an office. You could even telephone him there.

Owen entered the bar. A large figure seated on a stool turned to look at him. The man had wiry hair, graying now, and a florid face grown puffy with constant pickling.

Owen nodded toward a row of empty booths at the other side of the room. Russ gave an order to the bartender, slid off his stool and shuffled over to a booth, where Owen was already sitting down.

"How's it going, fella?" Russ's breath was heavy with alcohol. "How's the wife?"

"The wife is very well, thank you." Owen allowed a note of outrage to creep into his voice. The bartender brought their drinks, set them on cardboard coasters, and left.

Owen leaned across the table. "Who's this deputy of yours? I don't like him."

"Boyd Vinson. He's supposed to be good."

"Boyd Vincent? Is that a name?"

"Vinson. Vinson. He drinks a lot, but it makes him sharp, you know?"

"He's blowing the whole thing."

"Yeah, I know. He musta miscalculated on that hill, and then—"

"It should have been you. You've seen that hill. You'd have known."

"Yeah, I know that. I've got my reasons. This guy's supposed to be good. I don't know."

"He came to the hospital a few times. She recognized him. He blew it every time. Now I just got a call that she's been checking on my insurance."

"Oh . . . yeah."

"Where's this Vincent now?"

"I dunno."

"You dunno. That's great. Wake up, man, there's no more time. Why the f—" Owen looked around to see who might be listening. In his anger, he had let his voice rise.

"Why'd he have to come to the hospital, for chrissake? There's people all over there."

"Guess he wanted the rest of his money," Russ replied unhappily. "It can work. A lotta times—"

"The guy's an ape. He couldn't make anything work. Look, it's got to be today and it's got to be an accident. There's no more *time*, do you understand? You don't know where Vincent is. You're bombed yourself. Okay, forget it. Forget everything. Call him off. I'll have to do it myself." He finished the last of his drink and threw some money on the table to deprive Russ of the power of having paid for it.

"Now look," he said again as he stood up. "Forget it, you hear? Your friend Vincent can go to hell. And he can forget any ideas about talking. The police have a description, right? He got the first installment and he didn't deliver, so he can forget the rest. And you tell him to keep his mouth shut. He's dealing with a guy who's got ten times the brains he has."

Having made his point, Owen left the bar. He looked back once. Russ hadn't moved.

At least he hoped he had made his point. He shouldn't have said he was going to do it himself. But they'd figure it out anyway.

Where to now? He was formulating a plan. He'd have to pick up somebody. Some dupe. A sucker.

Somebody very young or very old. He thought of a Bowery bum, but that just wasn't likely. Anyhow, he was sick of lushes.

A young person. That'd work better. She might go for a young person. And it would have to be a naive person with no ties in the area. That let out a New Yorker on both counts.

Somebody who just arrived in town, looking for a job and a place to stay. Where did they come in? Not the airport, certainly. Probably not a train station, either.

Port Authority bus terminal. It was famous for those arrivals, exactly the kind he was looking for. He checked his watch—damn, it was getting late—hurried to the West Fourth Street subway stop and took an A train to Forty-second. He emerged in the lower concourse of the Port Authority terminal.

First thing, though, he had to get his kids out of the way. This might be dangerous. He didn't want to risk the kids either physically or emotionally. What happened to Tina had been bad enough. He found a pay phone and dialed the Elliotts in Great Harbor.

His first lucky break. Nancy picked it up herself. "Owen! Where are you calling from?"

He tried to shut out the noise of the terminal.

"I'm in the city. Can't get away right now, but listen, dear. Lyn was just in town. I don't think she could have gotten home yet. She was seeing her lawyer and didn't want me to know. I'm afraid she's trying to get the kids away from me. Once they're gone, I won't know where to find them, so will you do this? Will you meet their bus and keep them at your place? For the night, yes. Till I can get this straightened out. Your aunt and uncle won't mind, will they?"

She didn't think so. He told her not to mention the reason. He wished he could have thought of something better than this, especially in view of what was to come, but time was awfully short. He still had to find his dupe, and that might take a while.

He walked the length of the concourse, searching for the right type of person. He had heard they were an easy pickup. Drifting kids. Runaways. He saw lines of people waiting for outgoing buses, and others emerging from the dock of an incoming bus, but they all appeared to know where they were going.

He took an escalator to the main level. Maybe there would be a Traveler's Aid station. Maybe the bus offices would be a likely place. He tried to picture himself an adolescent who had run away from home and just arrived in a strange, teeming city. Where would he go?

But a late adolescent, he thought. It had to be plausible. And a late adolescent would not really be a runaway.

Just someone naive and confused. That was what he wanted.

Maybe that one there, with the too-short hair and the duffel bag. Could have been a serviceman coming home on leave, but he didn't look like a New Yorker. You could tell by his face. Not ethnic enough, or too open, perhaps. You could tell a Midwesterner from miles away.

Owen approached him and asked, "You just arrived in town, young man?"

The young man demanded belligerently, "What's it to you? Am I doing something wrong?"

Owen backed away. This was definitely not the one. He needed somebody who would trust him.

He saw another boy reading a Hagstrom map of the city. Not that, either. Not someone smart enough to buy a map and study it before venturing out onto the streets.

He continued to wander, feeling like an invisible man in the crowds, for he could inspect them at will and no one paid attention to him. He became more adept at spotting a likely target, watching for a while, and then rejecting.

Back to the lower concourse and another check of the arrival gates.

A bus was disgorging. Most of the people looked nondescriptly white. Probably a northern rural area. He stood back where he was inconspicuous, and watched.

Two young men. He wanted only one. But it turned out they were not together. One walked, beaming, into the arms of three women of varying ages. The other stood looking about as though wondering what to do. Finally he started toward the escalator. Owen followed, observing.

The boy was of medium height. Medium all around. Very forgettable. That was good. His face was uninteresting, his eyes blue and mild. Maybe even vacant. His dark hair waved in front and grew down to the collar of his jacket in back. Not bad looking, which was excellent for the purpose, and obviously no Einstein. That was even better.

At the top of the escalator, the boy paused to take stock again. His head turned this way and that. He seemed shaken by the immensity of the place. Owen moved in, barely remembering that he himself had no plausible reason for being in the bus terminal. Perhaps he wouldn't need one.

"Hi. You look lost. Can I help?"

"Yeah," said the boy. "Do you know where I can find a room?"

"You just arrived in town?"

"Yeah."

"Got a job or anything? Or are you trying your luck? Do you know anybody here?"

"No. Nobody. I'm going to look for a job tomorrow."

Owen edged him away from the escalator, so they would not obstruct traffic. "Any particular kind of job?"

"Whatever I can get."

Unskilled. This was turning out perfect. For Owen.

"I'll tell you," he said. "I live out on Long Island. About an hour, not too far from the city. I could use somebody to help around the place for a couple of weeks. My wife's been sick, and there's a lot of yard work, storm windows, and things. We could put you up. It would give you a chance to get your bearings. Where do you come from?"

"Otsego County. But, mister, you don't even know me. Would you trust somebody you don't know?"

Owen laughed. "If you ask if I can trust you, I'm pretty sure I can. And I think you have an honest face. The question is, can you trust me?"

The boy blinked, as though startled by the idea, and then smiled. "I guess so. Why not?"

Well, why not? He wasn't a girl, so nobody could force him into prostitution, right? And what else was there to worry about? Owen was satisfied. He had picked his mark unerringly.

They went out the Ninth Avenue exit and Owen hailed a taxi to take them to Penn Station.

"What's your name, by the way?" he asked, after the boy had absorbed his first view of an unprepossessing part of the city.

"Gary. Collier."

"Gary Collier? Mine's Holdridge. Owen Holdridge. What brings you to New York, Gary?"

"I thought I could make some money here. It's better than back home. We had a bottling plant, but it closed down. It was the only business in town. Now you can't get a job."

"How old are you?"

"Twenty."

"Really? I thought you were a little bit younger. Did you ever consider the Army?"

Gary shrugged, and then his attention was caught by the towers of Penn Plaza. "Wow!" he exclaimed.

"That's New York. A big, impersonal, uncaring city. You might have done better in the Army."

Owen could not resist his bit of philosophy as they left the taxi and entered the station.

He couldn't help a smile of satisfaction as his advice went unnoticed and unheeded.

It was too late for Gary now.

=24

On the train going home, she thought of Joe Singleton. Her mother had told her that, as far as she knew, he had never married again. In all those years, he had never married. Had she hurt him as badly as that?

It made her ache. He had been a good man, trying hard to build a life with her, and she had hurt him.

On the other hand, she never would have had the children if she had stayed married to Joe. Not Paul and Neal, but other children. She would never have known Paul and Neal.

Her plans were made. She would go straight home, pack a few things, take the boys, and leave. She could go to her mother's.

No, that would be the first place he would look. She could not even leave the children there while she went on. They would not be safe from him. Perhaps a motel.

But at a motel, her car would be parked in front like a banner, pointing to where she was. There were millions of motels, he would not know where to begin looking, but he might be lucky. His luck had always held before.

She could sell the car. She would need money, and the bank would be closed by the time she reached home.

The car was registered in his name. Only he could sell it.

She felt stifled in the train. She ought not to have come home at all, but she had to get the children. She couldn't leave them with him.

She should have stayed in the city. Found a job and a place to live, and picked up the children later. If he hadn't secreted them away by then.

It was too late now anyway. The train was pulling into Great Harbor station.

She drove home quickly. As she started to enter the house, Mrs. Sylvester blocked her way. "There's wet wax on the kitchen floor, missus."

"I have to get in. It's an emergency. Are the children home?"

"Just another minute. It's almost dry. The children came home, at least they got off the bus, and then this lady came in a blue car, and they drove up to the house, and one of 'em came in and asked if they could sleep over somewhere."

"*Where?* Did you find out where?"

"It was somebody they knew. Don't you worry, missus, they'll be calling you in a little while. It was a nice young lady with a little blue car."

"Did you talk to her?"

"Just for a minute. I stood in the door and she called out to me after they asked. She said, 'Is it all right?' I said I couldn't answer, they'd have to ask you, so they'll be calling." Mrs. Sylvester turned to survey the kitchen floor, and then graciously admitted her employer.

Lyn moved on legs that had gone numb. He couldn't have sent anyone to take the children. He wouldn't—

"What did she look like?"

"She was real pretty. Sort of blondish hair. You know."

Mrs. Sylvester's powers of description were scarcely adequate, but the words evoked an image. Nancy Lehrman.

But why? What was he doing? Could he possibly have found out about her inquiries?

Never from Mr. Brandon. It must have been Bill Stoddard. Or maybe he had only decided that this was the day.

"Are you feeling all right, missus?"

She tried to rally herself. "I'll be all right. It's just—"

She looked at the clock on the wall. Four-thirty. He would be home in about two hours. She hadn't time for a confrontation with Nancy. At least the children were safe where they were. But she was not safe. The danger could come from anywhere, at any time. He had hired the man with the winged eyebrows. He must have hired the man who killed Ruth.

The telephone rang.

"Mom?"

Neal or Paul, she could not tell which. "Mom, we're at Nancy's house. She wants us to sleep over."

"No!" shouted Lyn. "You come right back here this minute. It's the middle of the week. You can't sleep over on a school night. If she won't bring you, you'll have to walk. Both of you."

"Okay, Mom," said a subdued voice. "I didn't really want to stay here anyway."

So it was, as she had thought, a trick of his. They hadn't even wanted it. And it meant that something was imminent.

There was no time. If they didn't come back, she would have to leave without them. After she got established, she would hire a lawyer—

"I'll be going now, missus, if that's okay. I have to get to the store."

She had forgotten about Mrs. Sylvester. She would have to use some of her precious cash to pay her. It would only be decent to pay her for the rest of the week and tell her she would not be needed any more, but there wasn't enough money. Maybe she could send it later.

When the housekeeper had gone, Lyn hurried to her bedroom. She would need a few clothes. Most of all, she needed money. She would have to ditch the car and try to make it on her own. Everything that was small, that could be converted into cash, she threw into a bag with her clothes. Gold jewelry. A pair of diamond earrings. Her Christmas emerald. Two rare coins that belonged to Owen.

She hadn't time to get out the suitcases. The boys had a backpack. She stuffed it with their shirts, jeans, and under-

196

wear. At least it was spring. They would not need their heaviest clothing.

She had no idea where they would go. Someplace he would never think of. Kansas City or Houston. Chicago. Milwaukee. She wondered if her typing was still any good. She had forgotten most of her shorthand.

She was tying the flap on the backpack when she heard a car door slam. The children. She ran to the dining room and looked out of a window.

It was Owen.

He had come home early. Somebody was with him, a young man carrying a dilapidated brown suitcase. What did they plan to do?

She stood at the window. Trapped. Her heart pounded in her throat.

He would know she was home. Her car was out in front.

She heard the sound of the back door opening. She heard his voice. "Lyn? Lyn, honey, come and meet a friend of mine."

She did not move. He would come in and find her there, not moving.

"Lyn?"

She managed to reach the door into the kitchen. He saw her there and smiled. His companion stood beside him, a gangly young man with wavy hair and blue eyes. A mild man who seemed to wait patiently for someone to move him, as though he were a chess piece.

"This is Gary Collier," Owen said. "He's going to stay with us for a while and do some of the heavy work."

She started across the kitchen. She did not know whether to believe him or not. It was so extraordinary. A young man from nowhere.

"We still have Mrs. Sylvester," she said hoarsely.

"Mrs. Sylvester doesn't do yard work. And there are the storm windows and screens. I ran into Gary at Port Authority. He just came to town and was looking for a job and a place to stay. I thought this would be ideal."

She could see that Gary did not have winged eyebrows. He was not the man who had attacked her. Vaguely she wondered what Owen had been doing in the Port Authority bus station.

She was not sure whether she could trust him. He might be telling the truth. Perhaps she had been wrong about the whole thing.

Or maybe he had simply changed killers, because he knew she would recognize the first one.

Gary did not look like a killer. He looked like an innocent boy—which he may or may not have been.

But the children had been taken away. Remembering that, she was instantly on her guard.

She went through the motions. "Nice to meet you, Gary." She must have sounded frozen.

He smiled. One of his front teeth was slightly crooked. "Nice to meet *you*, ma'am."

Owen said, "Set down your bag, Gary, for heaven's sake. Is the spare room made up, Lyn?"

"I don't think so. If you'd called me, I could have had Mrs. Sylvester . . ." Her eyes turned away from meeting Gary's. Why should she make up a bed for someone who had probably come to kill her?

"Didn't think of it," Owen answered cheerfully. "Maybe you want to wash up?" he said to Gary. "Then we can all have a little drink and get acquainted."

"I don't drink, sir," Gary said.

Lyn could see that Owen was somewhat taken aback. Either the dialogue was an act, or he did not know Gary very well. She felt confused, vacillating between suspicion and trust. But she could not trust him completely, and so she must be ready for anything.

She led Gary to the den, which had two studio beds that were used for guests. It also had its own bathroom. Gary seemed awed by this luxury and by the size of the house in general. Again she wondered if Owen was on the level. No hired killer would be so blatantly unsophisticated.

Unless that, too, was an act.

After Gary had stowed his luggage, Owen took him on a tour of the house and grounds, showing him what needed doing.

They were in back of the house when the twins came up the driveway.

"We had to walk," Paul told his mother. "Nancy didn't want to bring us. She wanted us to stay."

They were here—and it was too late. But at least they were home.

"Maybe some other time," she said, scarcely hearing herself. Through a back window she could see Owen and Gary, deep in conversation, coming toward the house.

They reached the door. Owen was still talking, his hand on the knob. Neal asked, "What's for dinner?"

Owen looked up. He pushed the door open. She saw amazement wash over his face. Amazement and—She could not tell. She did not know what he was thinking. Almost immediately, he overcame his surprise.

"Well, hi, look who's here." His cheeks creased in that familiar smile. "My sons, Neal and Paul. Kids, this is Gary Collier, from upstate. He'll be staying with us for a couple of weeks and doing some work around the place." He turned to Lyn. "Honey, when's dinner going to be ready?"

She said, "I thought we were having a drink first."

"Let's have the drinks after. It's more relaxed that way. We don't want to keep the kids waiting for their food."

He seemed perfectly calm, perfectly reasonable. She could not understand what was happening. She lit the oven to warm Mrs. Sylvester's chicken casserole, and busied herself with setting the table.

She was not sure whether Gary, as hired help, would eat with them. Owen seemed to expect it. She set five places.

During dinner Owen was expansive and voluble, Gary silent and shy. The twins complained about the casserole.

Owen smiled pleasantly at Lyn. "And how did your day go?"

She was shocked, but quickly suppressed it. Her face had become stony during the evening. She must betray nothing.

"Okay, I guess."

"How's the hand?"

The twins both stopped eating to tell Gary what had happened to their mother's hand. Gary looked horrified. He mumbled something about New York. His family had advised him not to come.

"Oh, but that sort of thing could happen anywhere," Owen said. "People are getting more mobile and less moral." And he launched into a discussion of crime and greed and what he called the "me-first" morality.

Gary listened, fascinated. He seemed impressed by Owen. Perhaps, Lyn thought as she watched him, he really was just what he appeared to be—a naive kid. The whole thing was very bewildering.

She sent the children to their rooms to finish their homework while she cleared up from the meal and Owen talked on. The spring evening had long since faded into darkness. Gary was growing sleepy. He must have been tired from traveling all day. If, indeed, he had traveled all day. She wondered why Owen couldn't see that he was tired.

She checked on the children, allowed them half an hour of television, and told them to get ready for bed. In her absence the men moved to the living room, where she found them still talking.

Owen looked up as she entered. "Kids in bed?"

"Almost. And I think Gary—"

"Yes, I think we've worn Gary out. We'll have a little nightcap and then we'll all turn in. I'm sure we can use some relaxation first. How about the ice cubes, honey?"

Lyn went to the kitchen and filled an ice bucket. "We don't usually have ice with after-dinner drinks," she pointed out when she returned to the living room.

"These are our before-dinner drinks, but we're having them after," Owen replied. "I told you, we had to feed the kids. This way we can take our time and be civilized about it."

"Excuse me, sir, I don't drink," Gary reminded him.

"I have just the thing." Owen opened the cabinet he used as a bar and took out a bottle of Catawba grape juice.

"It's like wine, but it's nonalcoholic," he explained. "I give it to the kids sometimes. It's not chilled, but we have ice."

He poured a glassful and gave it to Gary, who studied and sniffed it, probably wondering if it really was nonalcoholic.

"I assure you, it's harmless," Owen said. He handed Lyn her vodka and tonic with the wedge of lime. All these years he had been making vodka and tonics for her, with a wedge of lime. All these years . . .

To Gary, she said, "Tell us about your trip. Was it very tiring?"

"Oh, no. It was a long trip, but I didn't get bored. I was looking out the window. There's a lot to see." He held up his glass and examined it again.

"Would you rather have something else?" Owen asked.

"No, this is fine." Eager not to offend, he took several large swallows.

Lyn began to feel easier. Perhaps it was the drink. Everything seemed to relax and smooth out inside her. Just as Owen said, a little relaxation.

I've got to go and see if the kids are in bed, she thought. Say good-night to them.

She did not want to move. She could sit here forever. Stay here forever.

She saw Owen as though in a dream, perched on the arm of a chair, regaling Gary with the story of some long-ago, eccentric tenant. Gary did not seem to be listening. They should have let him rest after that long bus ride.

"Maybe Gary would like a rest," she said.

But she hadn't said it. She only dreamed she had said it. Gary's chin dropped to his chest.

Owen was coming across the room toward her. For how long had he been doing that? He asked, "Are you all right?"

"I'm sleepy," she said.

"Well, you two are a handsome pair." He sounded disgusted. "Why don't you just go to bed?"

She would have liked nothing better. She tried to lie down on the sofa.

"Not here," he said. "This is no place for sleepy-bye. We have bedrooms for that." He pulled her to her feet.

She collapsed against him. "Can't walk."

"Then I'll have to carry you." He picked her up. So strong. Owen was so strong. She fell asleep in his arms and woke as he set her down on a bed.

She opened her eyes and saw that it was one of the studio couches in the den. "Mm?" she asked. She wanted to be in her own room, but could not get up. He was walking out and leaving her there. Her eyes fell closed.

She woke again as something tumbled onto the bed beside her. My God, it was the boy. Gary. Right beside her. She saw Owen bending over him, lifting his legs to the bed.

"No," she said. Not him. And it was too crowded.

"Go to sleep," Owen told her. "You'll both feel better after a little nap."

"Want my own bed." She was suddenly frightened.

Gently he pressed her head back to the pillow. "It doesn't make any difference, dear. You're both asleep."

She lay back and let her eyes close. It was too much trouble to argue. And then she slept.

When she woke the next time, Owen was sprinkling something onto the bed. She moaned and tried to sit up.

He said, "This is just to cool you off a little. It's kind of hot in here."

The room had an odd smell. She put her hand to her nose. "Stuffy." She could barely speak. Her tongue moved slowly.

"I'll turn on the air conditioner, okay?"

She noticed that the curtains were drawn. The windows

looked out on the back lawn, where no one could see in anyway. It all seemed very strange. She wanted to ask him why he was doing it, but lethargy gripped her. She could only close her eyes and sink again into sleep.

=25

The end of the fuse was in the kitchen. He had closed the blinds in that room and in the dining room. Anything showing around their edges would look, he hoped, like normal light.

He went back to the bedroom and changed into his pajamas. Took the bedspread off his bed. He felt like an actor setting a scene.

Only one thing was wrong. The children. They shouldn't have been here. He hadn't seen them when he first came home. He had thought everything was going smoothly. Of course it would look more natural with them here, but there was always a chance they might get hurt. Or wake up too soon and see what was happening. Hell, the best-laid plans . . . This wasn't even a best-laid plan, but it wasn't bad, considering how fast he'd had to come up with it.

Now he was ready for the big moment. Act Two: the kitchen. He crept back silently and listened outside the den door. Nothing. They were both out cold.

But not for long. Not cold for long. He smiled to himself.

In the darkness of the kitchen, he lit a match and held it to the fuse until it caught. Then he stood back to watch the tiny flame burn slowly along the string.

After a minute or so, he wrenched himself away. Had to be sure the boys weren't awake. He went back down the hall and looked in their rooms, first Paul, then Neal, opening their doors without making any noise. Both were sleeping soundly.

He stood in the hallway, listening. He could see nothing from there. But he had to know. Cautiously he tiptoed into the living room. The dining room.

He peered into the kitchen. The flame was still creeping up the fuse. He hadn't known it would take so long. It would be a while before he could logically get the children out. Damn, he hated this. Why did they have to be here? He went to his own room and sat on the edge of the bed. This was where he would normally be—although not sitting on the bed, but sleeping. He would have to do everything as normally as possible. Wait until exactly the right time. The moment when he would wake if he were asleep.

What if something went wrong? Christ, this was nerve-wracking. He wished it were later in the night so that fewer cars would be passing by. But he had kept his two pigeons up as late as possible, and he couldn't delay too long once they fell asleep. If only he'd had more time to arrange things.

He pictured himself waking the boys and hurrying them outside. Over and over again he imagined it. Would they be able to get out the front door? If not, maybe they could break a window. At least, thank God, they were all on the ground floor. In any case, they'd go out in front and stand on the lawn, so the children couldn't see what was happening. No point in scarring them for life. He would feel ridiculous out there in his pajamas. Would it make sense, he wondered, to put on a bathrobe? Would a person, caught by surprise, take the time?

Hell, had that fuse gone out? He opened his bedroom door. Nothing. Dark and quiet.

He tried to see out of a window. Unless he went into one of the boys' rooms, the other part of the house was hidden.

Damn, he had to know. He stepped into the hallway. The hinge squeaked on his door. He stopped. Mustn't wake the twins.

When he was sure he hadn't disturbed them, he began to move forward again. Into the living room. There, he caught a whiff of smoke. Or thought he did. On to the dining room.

He had closed the door to the kitchen. Now he saw light in the cracks all around it. He clutched at his heart. Had they gotten up? Impossible.

Then he realized what it was. He could hear it and smell it. He stood and stared, then hurried back to his room.

Still he could see nothing from there. He had planned it almost too well. He couldn't get the boys out yet. Not until it was evident in here. Not until it was so obvious that it would wake him, if he were asleep.

He could do nothing but sit and wait.

=26

She woke and stared at the ceiling. She felt hot. Terribly hot.

A brilliant streak flashed up onto the bed. She kicked at it and screamed. It rushed to embrace her.

She screamed again. Rolled to the floor.

"Help! Owen, help!"

The room was alive with fire. Strips of flame leaped across the carpet. She hugged her arms, trying to protect herself. She would be roasted alive. Already she could feel the heat, as though her skin were shriveling.

"Owen! Owen!"

The door. She staggered to her feet. The door.

A howl of terror. Someone was thrashing on the bed. She remembered—the boy.

"Get up!" she cried. His clothes were on fire.

She seized a pillow and beat at the flames. He grabbed her arm. His eyes were wild with fear. She felt herself pulled toward the bed.

"Get up!"

She wrenched free. Smoke clogged her throat. She couldn't breathe.

The boy writhed. Screamed. So young. Like Eddie. Dennis.

She half lifted him from the bed. Smoke filled the room and stung her eyes. The door—Where was the door? Nothing but smoke and fire. She coughed, fighting her way. The window.

She coughed. She would die, strangled in smoke. The boy weighed her down.

The window was on fire. Curtains burning. The air conditioner—damn air conditioner—The other window.

She had lost her bearings. Couldn't breathe. She choked and gagged on smoke.

She staggered. Tumbled into the burning curtains.

No. Can't die. Got to save Eddie. Neal and Paul.

She clawed at the curtain. It fell away. The window—locked. She beat at the glass. Her arm was too weak. She hit again.

Her head. Maybe her head.

The boy fell against her. Dying. They were both dying.

Her forehead hit glass. She felt it give way. She felt air on her face. Gulping for it, she swallowed smoke. The fire roared in her ears, searing her back.

Eddie.

He was a dead weight against her. Unconscious.

Got to save Eddie.

She pushed his head and shoulders through the window. Now lift.

Couldn't do it. He was too heavy.

She could leave him. Climb out herself. He wasn't Eddie, just a boy.

No, it wasn't fair. Not fair of Owen.

The boy moaned.

She lifted his feet. His knees. The ground below—it would break his neck.

With the last of her strength, she pushed him through.

Then she sagged to the floor under the window. Burning. Coughing.

"Hey, ma'am? Ma'am?"

The voice. He needed help.

She raised herself. Got to find Neal and Paul.

She slumped in the window, her arms scraped by broken glass. She could not move her legs.

The smoke burned through her. A blackness gripped her brain as she lost consciousness.

From his bedroom, with the door ajar, he heard a shout. He jumped from his bed and went out to the hall.

"Mom! Dad! A fire!"

Neal stood shivering in the doorway of his room. Shivering, not from cold, but with fear and excitement.

"A fire? Oh, my God!" He could see it through the window. Excellent. Excellent that it was Neal who discovered it.

He took command. "It's in the other wing. Go out through the front door. I'll get Paul."

"Aren't you going to call the fire department?"

"Neal, just *get out of the house.*"

Neal skittered down the hall in pajamas and bare feet. He would freeze. No time for coats.

Paul was asleep. Owen shook him awake. "Let's go. We've got to get out of here."

"Huh?" Paul responded groggily.

"Wake up, boy. The house is on fire."

"Where's Neal and Mom?"

Owen picked him up. He was almost too big to carry. "Go outside with your brother, so I know you're safe. I'll look for Mommy."

He felt a pang, calling her that. But the fire shouldn't have hurt her. She'd have been dead of smoke poisoning before she ever woke up.

They found Neal dancing on the lawn, his teeth chattering. "Can I get my coat? Where's Mom?"

"Stay here. I'll bring some blankets." Owen raced back into the house. There was not much chance the fire would spread this way for a while.

But when he returned with the blankets, both his sons were in tears.

"Mom! Where's Mom?"

He paused, aghast. Of course they would assume she had

been in the bedroom with him. He ought to have shown more concern.

"She fell asleep in the living room," he said. "I looked. She's not there now."

They started toward the door. He had to hold them back.

"I'll go and find her," he promised. "You stay right here. Don't move."

From far off, he thought he heard the sound of a fire whistle. It couldn't be for this fire. Not yet. Who'd have reported it?

Lights glimmered through the trees. With the leaves not fully out, even the people down over the hill could see his house.

He ran from room to room. He had to pretend to look for her. When he reached the dining room, he saw that the kitchen was engulfed. Smoke poured around the closed door into the rest of the house.

He wondered if the gas line would explode.

The boys clamored at the front door.

"Get back!" he ordered. "Get away from the house."

"Where's Mom?"

"She might have gone out. She might—"

They didn't believe him.

"She's in there," Neal cried, and tried to push past him. Owen blocked the way. They couldn't really know where she was.

"You stay here, guys," he said. "I'll go around—"

He heard it then. A siren. He began to shiver. He hadn't realized how cold he was in his pajamas.

"Stay right here." He hurried around the bedroom wing and across the barbecue terrace.

She woke again, feeling the heat. Above her the sky danced and the stars reeled. She lay on her back in cool grass.

She could hear it roaring. The fire. It was too close. She had to get away.

"Eddie?"

A whisper. That was all she could manage, just a whisper.

Something crashed nearby. Sparks burned her leg.

"Eddie!"

Then she saw him, crawling through the grass. She rolled away from the house. Rolled and rolled through the cool grass.

Safe. She was safe. She raised her head.

She stopped, frozen. Standing beside her, a pair of feet and legs.

"No!"

Only a whisper. She couldn't move. He seized her wrists. She gasped in pain.

He began to drag her across the grass. He couldn't leave her alive. She twisted and kicked as he pulled her toward the fire.

She tried to scream. She screamed a whisper. There was no one to hear.

Owen! No!

Don't hurt her, he had said. *Not into the fire.*

"Mom! Mommy!"

She heard their voices. Got to save—Neal and Paul.

For just a moment, he hesitated. "Get back, kids."

"What are you doing to Mom?"

"*Go back.*"

She twisted again, trying to pull free. She had to save them. Get them away from the fire.

"Dad?" An urgent voice. Terrified. They had seen what he was doing.

She strained her throat. "Neal . . . Paul . . ."

A flicker of new fire. They were cut off. Trapped.

No—it was a flashing red light. Dark figures rushed across the barbecue terrace.

Then shock waves of heat struck her as the roof fell in on the den.

=27

Again she lay in the hospital, voiceless.

But she could whisper. She had been able to tell them about the fire.

He, in turn, said that he had been trying to save her, to pull her from the flames. He said they had all been in the living room having a drink, and then he had gone to bed, leaving his wife and the new handyman together. He never imagined— But she had been drunk, he said. They must have gone to the den together. Probably she had been smoking on the bed . . .

She was afraid they would believe him. But there were witnesses. There were Neal and Paul. And Gary. She wondered how Gary was feeling. She remembered his name now. He wasn't Eddie.

Poor boy. His first day in New York. It wasn't fair of Owen.

But he was alive. And Owen? They had arrested him right there on the back lawn. In his pajamas. She did not know where he was now.

She had loved him once.

Suddenly she tensed. Footsteps paused outside her door. She reached for the call button. She looked about for something to throw, anything that would make a noise. The tray, the pitcher, drinking cup—they were all plastic. Too quiet.

Someone was coming in. She tried to raise herself to her elbow, but her arms were burned and bandaged. She held her thumb on the call button—

Joe Singleton!

He stood awkwardly in the doorway, clutching a bouquet of roses in one hand.

"Hi, Lyn."

She whispered his name. They stared at each other. Fourteen years.

"Smoke in your throat?" he asked. She nodded.

He held out the roses. "I brought you some flowers." She nodded again.

He sat down in the chair beside her bed. She could not get over it. Joe Singleton.

"How did you know?" she asked in a strained whisper.

"It was in the papers."

"All of it?"

"Enough."

Enough so that he knew most of the story. She wanted to talk, and tell him what happened. To tell him that he still looked the same, only maybe a little older. But not fourteen years older. To tell him she was sorry.

She put her hand to her throat.

He said, "I missed you, Lyn."